For Judy –
many good memories–
Sallie Bingham
July 14, 1993

# *UPSTATE*

A NOVEL BY

Sallie Bingham

THE PERMANENT PRESS
Sag Harbor, New York 11963

**Library of Congress Cataloging-in-Publication Data**

Bingham, Sallie.
    Upstate / by Sallie Bingham.
        p.    cm.
    ISBN 1-877946-33-8 : $21.95
    I. Title.
PS3552.I5U6   1993
813'.54—dc20              92-34345
                            CIP

Manufactured in the United States of America


THE PERMANENT PRESS
Noyac Road
Sag Harbor, NY 11963

# 1.

I am standing on Shultz Hill at six o'clock in the morning: Labor Day. To the west, the Hudson River Valley is streaked about equally with industrial smoke and fog. The river itself is hidden by a fold of hills. Beyond it lie the Catskills, those humpbacked purple mountains, which we never climbed in our eight years here. To the east, the Berkshires back up against a cloudbank which is reddened by the hidden sun. At my feet, the little hills and valleys of my country are lined with banners and processions of mist. It is an old, failed landscape, the farms gone—my place was one of them—and the fields grown back with sumac, heaven trees and scrub pine. Even on my hilltop, I can hear the buzz of early-morning traffic to Poughkeepsie.

Eight years ago, I bought the white house which I can see in the valley: a small frame house, with eight rooms divided four downstairs and four up. It was the cheapest advertised that Sunday in the "Farms and Country Homes" section of *The New York Times.* Waiting for the real estate agent to unlock the door, I heard the traffic on the highway, beyond the yard and a row of old maples. I was carrying Jeff, and Molly and Keith were picking along behind me. "You do hear the road," my husband observed.

"That's just 11H," the real estate lady said, "an old two-laner they'll never get around to widening. You can't actually see it from the house."

A few hours later, I had decided to buy the house, with money my grandfather had made off railroads in Florida.

"Do you want it?"

"Yes. Do you want it?"

"Yes. But you do hear the highway . . ."

I was a righteous person, working on my third baby, protecting my two older children from most of the rigors of the world and satisfying my husband to the best of my distracted ability; fortunately his demands were minimal. I had packed my life so tight there was no room for one alien impression, one mistaken impulse to intrude. So buying a house on whim was like buying a mad hat or a chocolate ice cream cone: it just didn't fit.

The sun moves up out of the cloudbank, blinding me and casting my stork-tall shadow across the grass. A blue-jay screams in the woods behind me. The grass as it warms smells sweet. Across the river, the trees shimmer and turn green and the traffic on the highway picks up. It is morning, time to go home.

I turn down the path. The first climb, and the last. At eight o'clock, the auctioneer and his men are coming to set up their tent in my yard. We are selling eight years of accumulation— "household effects," the advertisement called it—because the house has been sold and we are moving on.

We?

I think of the children sleeping, each in his cell. Their light breath fills the house, lifting it slightly, ballooning out the thin frame walls.

My husband is here, too, for the auction, installed in the downstairs guest room. We have been married for fifteen years and separated for the last five months. His hairbrush and shaving gear are laid out on the toilet tank in the bathroom, as neatly aligned as they were on the shaky nightstand, in Florence, in the room where we spent our first careful, sticky night. He had a zip-up bag which contained all the necessities, even a pack of rubbers which he slipped under the pillow, not quite escaping my eye. Those were the old days, and my diaphragm had stayed in my pensione with my guide books and camera and list of letters to write home.

Walking down the hill, I wonder why my children have never seemed as young as David and I seemed, that summer in Florence and for so many years afterwards.

I stop at the edge of the highway, feeling self-conscious in my rubber boots and old Mexican serape. Pale faces peer from the interiors of speeding cars. At last I cross, at a dead run. I hurry up the gravel road, wondering what David will think if he wakes up and finds me gone.

I crossed the patch of parched grass between the concrete slaughterhouse and the sideporch. My begonias are bloom-

ing in crocks on either side of the door. I slide it back and
step into the smoke from burning pancakes. David is stand-
ing at the stove in his white pajamas, pouring batter onto the
griddle. He glances at me, smiles, and pours another dab.
"Good morning, Ann. Enjoy your walk?"
I grunt. His civil behavior is a cross I will not bear.
"The children are still asleep," he says.
"They wouldn't be frightened if they woke up and found
I wasn't in bed. They know I take walks in the early morning."
"Would you like some pancakes?"
"No, thank you."
"I put blueberries in them." He is proud of his newly-
acquired cooking skill. I am thinking of the price of the blue-
berries, charged to my account at Mrs. Hunter's fancy fruit
market.
"You sound like a teenager."
"You put me in my place." I push my heel into the crude
wooden bootjack which Edwin and his eldest son made for
me, last Christmas. Stepping on the back of the jack with my
other foot, I imagine that I am stepping on David's neck.
"I see you still have that thing," he says, sitting down to his
pancakes. His pajama fly gapes and I catch sight of a mass
of dark curled hair. He closes his fly with one hand, then
pours maple syrup liberally on his pancakes. "I thought you
said you were going to get rid of it."
"It has been in and out of the garbage several times."
Watching him eat, I am annoyed by his silent assumption: he
has always said that Edwin caused it all. "I am going to keep
everything he gave me," I add defiantly. We both know there
is nothing else.
I hang the bootjack on its nail and stop its swinging, gently,
with my hand. Edwin's handiwork. Why is it that making love
once with Edwin under a full moon in a wet field mattered
more to me than fifteen years of discussion, dinner parties,
agreement, affection, shared meals, plans, children? Edwin,
the maker, with his small strong hands, the opposition between thumb and forefinger maddeningly delicate, precise.
Edwin, the wizard, the healer, the one who splits the soul.
David eats, his fork traveling to his mouth at regular inter-
vals. Now and then he wipes his lips with a folded paper
napkin. He has set the sugar bowl where he can reach it next
to the vitamin pills, lined up silverware on either side of his

mat. Next to his right hand, he has laid a yellow legal pad and a sharpened pencil; I see the date written across the top.

"What are you going to write on your pad?" I ask.

"Just a few thoughts. When are they coming to set up the tent?"

"In half an hour, at eight. Tom wants to have everything set up and ready to start the auction at ten."

We both glance into the living room where the furniture is huddled in a corner. "I notice you've decided to sell your aunt's sewing table," David remarks. "It's very fine. Don't you think you ought to keep it for the children?"

"I've told you several times, I'm keeping almost nothing."

"It seems to me you ought to keep something from your family, for the children." He catches a runnel of maple syrup on the side of his fork and carries it to his mouth.

"What are you keeping from your family?" I ask.

"Nothing, really. I don't like that heavy Victorian stuff. My mother asked for the pair of Ming lamps—I told her I'd see to it that she gets them."

"Be sure to put a label on them."

"I will, as soon as I'm finished here. Surely you're going to keep the grandfather clock?"

"I don't think the children are going to want a grandfather clock."

"Why should you decide for them?"

"They can have my diaries," I say, "when they want them. That's the whole story: money and desolation. The furniture, the silver, the china—that's the trimmings."

"I don't like yard sales."

"This isn't a yard sale, it's a cut higher—an auction. The last yard sale was a disaster." I like to make concessions when I can. "People parked all over the grass and they wanted to see what else we had in the house."

"That woman from Red Hook came into the parlor and actually asked me the price of the chair I was sitting on."

"You were very polite, you even offered her a cup of coffee."

We laugh and the weight lifts. I go on eagerly, "It was a real disaster, a mistake in judgment. Do you remember, it began to rain after lunch and we had to haul everything inside. We only made something like nine dollars, and that had to be divded among the three children." I do not remind him that I was helpless with giggles all day, rattling my change box like a leper's bell.

Since then I have wanted to get rid of the rest of my possessions. When David moved out, my wish began to grow vigorously, sprouting roots and leaves like the sweet potato vine I grew in a glass jar as a child; now the roots have filled all the available space. I am bound to my mistakes by these chairs and tables, these nesting ashtrays and mismatched lamps, all remnants of other pasts, some mine and now partially detached, some connected to other people's lives. It seems to me that change will come more quickly without the framework of my mother's good taste and my own extravagance, David's mother's vulgarity and his own cleverness at spotting a good buy.

I imagine the way the living room will look, cleared out, full of sun, as it was when I first saw it. I am making space here, again, I am clearing the way. I am also hoping to make a little money. With it, I will be able to buy the essentials for the apartment in the city where I will be living alone with my two younger children.

I look into the living room again. My family's things—the sideboard from the Georgia house, the Shaker rocking chair, the cradle we never used—are pushed together with the carved wooden knicknack shelf, the icon with its starring eyes and the curly-legged rosewood chairs which David's mother contributed. Around and beneath these objects lie the things we bought ourselves—the little round mirror from the antique store in Claverack, the toolchest the children used for blocks. All these things have fused into a molten lump.

I remember unlocking the front door on winter Fridays, my arms full of groceries, the children scrapping at my heels; the furniture loomed in the dark like the real inhabitants of the place. The overstuffed chairs by the fireplace were as gross and misshapen as the farm wives whose yearly labors took place in the downstairs guestroom, the china cabinet loomed like a maiden aunt. I only loved the house in the beginning, when it was nearly empty. Then there was the sweet smell of baby powder, the fragrance of the pine essence I used in the vaporizers, the fine stink of diapers. As the children began to grow up, the house began to fill with things, and then the parties began.

Last New Year's Eve, I sat on the basement steps with Edwin, his cool hand down the back of my jeans. Looking down, I saw a cow snake lying on the warm cement next to the furnace. "Look at the snake," I said. Edwin got up, went down the steps, took up the broom and, with a whack, broke the snake's back. Then he opened the basement door and scraped the snake out, where it lay in a loop on top of the frozen snow. "You should really have kept it to eat the mice," he said, coming back, the cold air fresh in his dark hair. Sitting down again beside me on the stairs, he put his hand again down the back of my jeans; his fingers were chilly.

Now Edwin and I do not see each other anymore and I do not know what to do with what I have become. In six years of living alone, I've seen enough to know that my careful opposites at dinner parties will never want my hunger. Even Edwin had his doubts, calling me names when I was too greedy. He did not believe me when I told him I loved him. He had only his penis to offer and he wanted to be accepted for that alone; but also to be honored as a friend, revered as a doctor, appealed to as an authority on the problems of childhood, respected in general for his commitment, his moral stance. The split in this man was so wide and so deep that my ceaseless attempts to bridge it were as futile as a spider's aim to fling a thread from one fence-post to the next—not that a spider would have tried. Yet my split man is the only man in the world who seems worth reassembling, to me, or loving in pieces (he would say, to pieces), the only man in the world whose honest pain cannot be comforted, whose rage cannot be placated, who exists independently of my love and attention (although not of his wife's) like a meteor on a dark country night.

David has taken his plate to the sink. "I think you're making a mistake with this auction," he calls over the running water.

I walk over to him, realizing as I do that there is a space of inert air, as resistant as plastic, between us. "We talked about this months ago, David. I told you then I wanted to get rid of practically everything."

"I don't believe you can do it."

"I know. Also I need the money."

This is something he will not discuss. He squeezes soap onto the dishes.

"When are you going to decide how much you can afford to give me for the children?"

"My lawyer is talking to your lawyer next week. I doubt if you're going to clear very much on this auction, by the time we've split the proceeds and paid the expenses. Labor Day—whose idea was that?" For the first time, he is crisp.

"Tom thought it was a good idea—the end of the summer, people feeling restless, ready to buy. He should know, I thought."

"Tom? Well, he's in the business. I never have heard anything good about him, though. He has those auctions in that rundown inn in Hillsdale, doesn't he?"

"Yes, those and that one which was really quite good—the Hull place on the river."

He is mollified. "Still, I would have thought Labor Day was a bad time to choose, especially with this weather. People are going to the lake."

"We'll just have to see, won't we?" My tone has become the nasty harsh self-justifying voice I used with my children when they were too young to argue.

Attracted by my sharpness, he asks, "How are you managing, living alone? Are you all right?"

He is coming with the bandages.

"I like it a great deal. I've always liked living alone. The year before we were married, when I was working in New York, was one of the happies times of my life." That of course is not entirely untrue. I add, "Being up here alone for eight summers with the children was what convinced me I wanted to live by myself."

"I don't know how you can say that."

"Well, it's so, in a way. The more conspicuous reason may turn out in the end to have been less important."

His eyes slide around the curve of my cheek before catching on my ear; they hang there briefly while he speculates. "Don't you think it might have been worth something,—another year, or so?"

"I don't know. Nothing would have changed."

He gets up to let in the cat who is scratching at the kitchen door. He waits until she has finished rubbing against his legs and then sits down so that she can jump onto his lap. "It might have changed," he says.

"Why? You weren't hurting, and I was half asleep."

"I was starting to notice a little something."

I laugh, hear the teetering sound and stop. "A little something. Such as that we never wanted to fuck anymore. When I used to try to talk about it, you'd say I was being pessimistic."

"You were always so black. You never wanted to talk about the good things."

"What were they?"

He stirs sugar into his coffee. "It's late to talk about that now. First you made up your mind you want a separation and now you want an agreement, as well."

"I thought you wanted it, too—to straighten things out."

"I told you, if you want it, I'll agree. If you want a divorce, I won't fight it."

"Anything I say. Why is it I'm not worth a fight?"

"Because you've already made up your mind," he says.

And yet I want him to fight for me, to struggle against the current that is sweeping us apart.

After a pause, David asks, "Where are the children?"

"They'll be up soon." I know he has reached the limit of his endurance; the children will provide a little padding. How easy it is, still, for me to read his signs. David's mother, the dragon lady, used to ask me why I couldn't understand her son; she had taught him a set of signals which worked quite well in the rest of the world, worked superbly well, in fact, in his law firm and at dinner parties. I tried to explain that I could read him well enough but that his vocabulary was too limited. My own is simplified enough, but it is entirely different. It is only in the last year that I have been forced to add a few qualifiers to what is, after all, only the old sordid all-engulfing search for love. Now I know that I must also learn to survive, and that is another language.

"There they are," David says. I think he means the children, then see that he is looking out the window. Tom's green pickup has turned onto the gravel road. It stops at the slaughterhouse and two men climb out. "I wonder if we ought to offer them coffee," David says.

"I don't think they expect it."

David goes to the window to watch them. The two men let down the truck's tailgate and begin to haul out a mound of canvas.

"What percentage are they getting?" David asks.

"The usual."

"What," he asks quietly, "is the usual?"

"I've forgotten. You can ask Tom when you take him out the coffee."

"I'm not going to take them out the coffee. This is another example of the way you got your finances into such a mess: you simply don't remember detail."

"I thought they were your finances, too."

"You were handling the money, paying the bills," he says wearily, having been over the ground too many times.

"But you still haven't told me what happened to your salary, all those years, or why you kept it in a separate account."

"I've explained as well as I can. You are determined as far as I can see not to understand. I told you about the expenses for the house, the mortgage . . ." Catching my eye, he turns abruptly away. "I'm going upstairs to dress."

He walks off rapidly, unbuttoning his pajama jacket. Before I have to remind him, he remembers that he is no longer sleeping upstairs and turns into the guest room.

How well-mannered he is, how discreet, still, even in the midst of what I must assume is outrage and resentment. He will never look at me with fury or abuse me; he will maintain our calm, and I will always feel something of a fool as I flounder and toss in it. Of course he has explained everything—but when?—and of course I have failed in the whirlwind of my resentment to listen, to understand. I have always been distracted by my sense of what he leaves out.

His explanations remind me of my mother's lectures on sex, illustrated with a photograph of the naked Perseus, in my book of Greek myths. I paid more attention to the snakes, writing around Medusa's face. It is the snakes which are always left out in these explanations—the rage, the disappointment, the slithering and unfolding of revenge.

# 2.

September, a year ago: a fusty Saturday, full of woodsmoke and the threatening claustrophobia of early fall. During the morning, the sun burned through layer after layer of mist. By the time David and I had been to town to buy the groceries, *The New York Times* and the pots of chrysanthemums, the day had turned hot and the children were complaining because the swimming pool had already been covered.

We unloaded the station wagon, each child agreeing to carry something, which turned out to be a jacket. There were, as always, six brown bags of groceries to take into the house. David and I hauled them in and began putting everything away, opening cabinet doors into each other's faces. We were both perfectionists and would have preferred to do the job alone. I stacked a can of chicken soup on top of one of David's pyramids and the whole thing collapsed, cans rolling off the shelf, one of them bouncing on David's toe. "Ow ow ow!" I shouted, hopping on one foot, but he smiled his enigmatic smile and picked up the cans and began to rebuild his pyramid on a wider base.

Molly and Jeff careened through the kitchen, firing the capguns David had bought them in lieu of allowance.

I screamed, "Get out of here!" David said something soothing. "Why do you buy them capguns?" I asked. "You know I can't stand the noise."

"They wanted them."

"What if they had wanted dynamite?" I began to lecture to tone down my irritation. "Shooting capguns is one thing they don't need to be taught. Everything else—books, models, all the worthwhile things—mean one or the other of us has got to help. We never help them anymore, have you noticed? Neither of us seems to have the patience." I was growing calm, having shouldered half the blame.

"I help Keith with his homework."

"I mean, things they do with their hands. They don't know how to put anything together or even take it apart; Keith asked me the other day to screw a lightbulb into his desk lamp. They don't seem to understand how things fit together, and now they've given up even asking for help so we won't be irritated. They just do what they can do alone. They seem to accept the fact that we're both permanently distracted."

"They all do well in school."

"Maybe because it's all abstract, or because they can ask for help there." Suddenly I tasted my fatigue, the sourness of the last late night in the back of my throat. "All we do here is go to parties."

"Helena was expecting us, last night. She would have been upset—"

"I know. There are always reasons, good reasons. But we came here in the beginning to be quiet, to be with the children, and now we're never with them. Mrs. T. has to come on Friday and spend practically the whole rest of the weekend here." I was bargaining on the fact that David would not mention that it was I who accepted all the invitations.

"If you don't want to go to Saul's birthday party—"

"That's different," I interrupted hastily.

David did not ask me why.

I went on in the humming voice of perpetual strain. "Sometimes I wonder if they are going to grow up just heathen—the children—or simply unskilled, manual illiterates."

"I don't see what that has to do with our going to parties."

The children streamed through again.

"Get out of here with those guns!"

Giggling, they fled outside, slamming the door.

"Is it a perpetual fantasy?" I asked David.

"Maybe. Let's get those chrysanthemums out."

We went back to the car; I waited while David brought the old red wheelbarrow. Together we loaded the six pots of shrysanthemums. David took up the handles and began to trundle the wheelbarrow down the hill to the flower garden. We'd arranged it badly, the weight was all to the front, and the wheelbarrow began to lumber rapidly, jerking David along. "Watch out!" I shouted. The wheelbarrow toppled over on the hill, one clumsy leg sticking up into the air. The chrysanthemums bowled out. David began to pick them up, breaking off the bent branches and laying them in a little pile. I was furious. The branches reminded me of the limbs of children, neatly stacked. I went to help David and even apologized for loading the wheelbarrow badly—anything to avoid a fit of rage, which would have left me sweating and trembling in the void of David's calm.

We carried the plants to the edge of the flowerbed; David took up the shovel. With its edge, he began to feel for a giving place in the gravel. We had ordered the garden to be made in the foundations of the fallen-down barn, and the gardener, taking advantage of our ignorance, had added a bare two inches of topsoil to make the beds. There were rocks everywhere under the briefly flourishing plants; they dried up and died in a hot summer. Each spring, we replanted, at great expense, since the frost heaved up most of the perennials. The garden was our most successful creation, radiant with tulips and daffodils in May, a scorched desert of drooping petunias in July. Now it had entered its empty period, which the chrysanthemums would disguise. Behind the singed petunias, in front of the iris, David found a spot that gave and began to dig a small hole.

I began again to gnaw at my subject. "You know, David, sometimes I think we only come to the country to see the Fields."

"It is lucky for us they are here. Our kids get along so well."

"They're not really friends, though, have you noticed? Except for Jeff and Saul. The others just hang around together. It's the grownups, really who enjoy each other."

"Yes. It works very well." He took one of the chrysanthemums and edged it into the hole, which was too shallow.

"You'll have to dig more," I said.

He lifted the plant out and began to pry at the hole with the shovel. "I'm afraid I've hit rock," he said after a while.

Crouching down, I felt the dry earth at the edge of the rock. I began to claw away at it, my nails clogging as the dirt piled up; as a child, I had clawed the dirt at home to get rid of the new feeling after my grandmother cut my nails. "Here, use the trowel," David said, dismayed, but I continued to rake with my nails at the dirt. At last I uncovered the rock and lifted it out, straining. It was flat and wide, an oldtime occupant, nearly a foot across. I hoisted it up, longing to hurl it, but it was too heavy; I staggered to the edge of the flowerbed and dropped it with a thump in the long grass.

"Good for you," David said. He sunk the plant into the deepened hole and began to stamp the dirt around it.

"Do you think we've learned anything about plants, in eight years?" I asked when I had my breath back.

David paused to consider the situation. "Yes, I believe we have. The catalogues are very helpful."

"We haven't learned much about anything else."

"I don't know what you mean."

I did not have the courage to go on. Digging in the earth had reminded me of sex. Sweating and straining generally did, as though physical effort was the most important component of fucking: simply the effort required to lift the arms and legs, tilt the pelvis and rotate the hips, combined with the more obscure but equally arduous effort required to lift a flagging penis. David and I had begun several years before to ration this effort. We did not sweat together now, in bed, unless we had the electric blanket turned too high, yet it was exhaustion which provided us, finally, with the excuse to stop fucking altogether. For six months, we had rested, hoarding our energy for a later day. All in all, it was a relief. Looking back, it seemed that the exercise had never been worth the effort, raising hopes for intimacy which were certain to be dashed. I had never come with David and he had stopped coming with me; this underground blight had finally attacked our affection. David was parching me, leaching me dry as I was parching him. He did not give me money and he did not give me his prick; the connection was as odious as it was vital. That he was a good father, in his absent way, and a decent man no longer mattered to me at all.

"I'm not going to be able to stand it much longer," I said.

He unpotted the next plant with a tap. "What?"

I did not answer and he did not ask again. We had both learned to avoid questions which had no ready answer.

Instead, I turned away. "It's nearly noon, I'm going to get the children ready for the party."

"All right. I'll come up to the house in five minutes."

Walking up the hill, I began to imagine Saul's birthday party and my anger evaporated. I knew I would see Edwin there, possibly touch him, possibly steal a word or two alone. We would be able to plan our next meeting.

I lifted my head and looked around for the first time that day. The willow behind the house was yellow, its streamers separated by sharp lines of shadow. Growing over the cesspool which it clutched with its roots, the willow sprang a few feet higher every year, clearing the peak of the house. It had been planted by a second wife, two generations ago.

Behind the willow, my land fell away into a shaggy, overgrown field, full of straggling hay which was bleached now and bowed to the ground. Goldsmith had refused to cut it this year, saying it wasn't worth his time. It worried me to see the land lying idle, growing up with milkweed and cockleburs, but I did not have the money to pay Goldsmith—he had taken the hay before as a fair exchange—and I knew the time had come for me to accept, as my neighbors had, that the land had lost its primary use. Next summer, there would be sumac in the field; the year after, scrub pines. The pasture would cease to have any justification except as a backdrop for our lives.

Beyond the field, a low limestone ridge marked the boundary of my land. Keith had found an old dump back there. He had come running into the house to tell us that he had uncovered all sorts of treasures, including a doll buried to her waist in the dirt. A grey day, with some rain; we all rushed back to see, but when we pulled the doll out of the dirt, we saw that her legs were eaten through. She had kept, in her obliterated face, a lipstick smile—a dead toy, abandoned one or two years ago with the mottled tin coffee pot and the busted buckets.

I saw the children running from underneath the willow, running in all directions, as though they had been exploded. "Time to go to the party!" I shouted. Suddenly, by one of those changes which made my life, in spite of everything a curiosity and a delight, I was pleased with it all—the close smoky day, the house, the life I had laboriously made around children and dinner parties and the conversation of friends, all illuminated now by my secret life with Edwin.

Jeff came running toward me, and Molly and Keith followed behind. I had the uncomfortable feeling that the older two had been talking. They did not play anymore, turning that activity entirely over to Jeff; instead, they talked, and refused to share their long half-whispered conversations. I suspected them of analyzing. At least Jeff had not outgrown his games. "They hid from me!" he whined, coming so close to me his face nudged my side; I imagined a calf butting its mother's bag, getting down to the business of nursing. I turned away, ignoring him. "You're not listening," Jeff complained.

"I'll listen when you tell me something I want to hear,' I told him, catching his hand and pulling him towards the house.

At the porch door, I looked back and considered them separately. Three children, all inconceivably mine, they clustered close to me to complain. Keith was looking, as always, sour and fat; at thirteen, he had lost his bones, and his shirt buttons strained across his plump chest. Molly was wearing one of his shirts and a pair of his jeans which hung loose from her hips; she was only ten and she had not yet given up her hope of being transformed into a brother—not a boy plain, but a boy caught and held in the mystical union of brotherhood. She refused to wear anything except Keith's clothes, maintaining her faith in flys and leather belts and torn striped jerseys which showed her staring breastbone. A beautiful girl, a little witch, the source of my undoing—as sometimes I thought when I saw her perched on Edwin's lap. She was the only one of my children he liked and she liked him, too. All the girls' mothers I knew joked about their daughters' seductiveness, yet it still seemed strange to me that Molly was so flirtatious when she genuinely, painfully wanted to be a boy. The two wishes—to seduce, and to be seductive— were after all perhaps not contradictory, perhaps not even connected at all. Edwin responded to her, feeling her round bottom gently with his hands, as though she were a precious bauble dangling on a thread. Perhaps, after all, this was what Edwin wanted, this little-girl's body possessed by an overriding hope that it was male. Because of that hope, anything could be done to Molly, any opening entered: she was by her own will androgynous.

Jeff, whining along behind, looked like a pale blond ghost with his cobwebbed blue eyes and his shaggy head. His last hysterical fit at the barber's in New York had convinced me never to have his hair cut again. David was supposed to do it at home, but since he was opposed to anything that smacked of force, he was not going to do it and I would have to cut Jeff's hair eventually myself. I would not have minded cutting it if it were not for his screams; my own child staring at me panic-stricken. He had the same fear of being seen naked. At school, he went through elaborate contortions in the bathroom, hiding his genitals behind a towel, and when it was time to change for gym, he had permission to go and lock himself in the supply cupboard. Otherwise he would not go to gym. These concessions sealed his disability. I imagined him as an old man, shielding himself in men's rooms, trying to explain with a joke that he had never, in seventy-three years, been seen without his pants.

It was easier, although I worked harder, when they were small; then their needs were clear and mostly connected with feeding and elimination. Sometimes still I cleaned their nails with my nail or inspected their ears or tried to catch them on my lap, but mostly, they grew like cabbages, flourishing in my distraction, in some rich soil of their own invention. Only the new closeness between Molly and Keith alarmed me. When I heard them whispering together, I longed for the evil days when Keith had hated his new baby sister and had walked the house at night, howling, clutching his ears, wetting his bed when I forced him back into it and then screaming at the sight of the dark patch on the sheet. With Molly goggleheaded in the shoulder sling, I'd held Keith in my arms, trying to quiet him when my own arms were stiff as pistons with resentment, when he must have felt, in my soothing hands, the clutch that would have torn his hair out if I'd lost control. David was away that summer, working on the provisions and charters for an Arabian bank, and I was more proud than angry to be left with it all. David's contribution had always been minimal. I had wanted it that way. The babies had needed me, separately, completely, devouring whole areas of my attention and patience until there was not an inch left for my discontent to sprout. All I had wanted, those first years, was to get from one day to the next, or possibly, to sleep through the night; as soon as Molly was out of diapers, Jeff had come along. Devoured, devouring, I was satisfied for a long time with the awe I inspired as the singlehanded homemade mother of three small children.

"I wish you'd get some help," my mother had observed on one of her whirlwind visits from Florida. She'd brought me a bright pink dress which I was too thin and too pale to wear. I did not try to explain to her that I would never give over even a tiny piece of my children; after all, they were all I had. On evenings in the city when David and I went out, I was pleased if the telephone-ordered sitter proved to be ugly or old; the children would not like her. Now, of course, if Edwin had been free in the evening, I would not have cared whether or not the children fell in love while I was away.

We crowded onto the porch. "I wish you children would wash your faces and brush your hair before you go." I said, realizing too late that I had put in exactly the inflection which would allow them to refuse.

"My hands are already clean," Molly said.

Keith, in parody, waved his hands in my face; they were enormous, the half-inch long nails lined with dirt.

Jeff grumbled, "Last year you made us put on all clean clothes for Saul's party and we were the only clean ones there."

I laughed. "Last year you were all a year closer to babies; I wanted you to look nice." Last year, I might have added, I did not much care how I looked myself. Now the time I would have spent on getting the children ready could be spent on my own decoration. "I'm going to change and I don't want to be bothered," I announced, marching off towards the stairs.

The children went into the kitchen and began to open and close the cabinets. "No eating!" I shouted down the stairs, knowing how wounded Flora would be if they turned down her spaghetti.

Upstairs in the bathroom, I spread the bathmat on the muddy floor (there was never time to clean the house, and we existed, quite happily, in dirt) stripped off my denim shirt and washed myself, shivering, from the waist up. The house did not warm up or dry out from October until May; even with the windows open all weekend, there wasn't time to get rid of the sour damp smell which had accumulated during the week. For generations, the house had been crammed with people—relatives, farmhands, an occasional boarder; the big locks on all the inside doors told of their need for privacy. The men had worked on the farm, the women had cooked and cleaned and raised children, and the house had never been empty or quiet or arranged or decorated. It had been a funnel, a shoot to the outdoors, or a protection from it. How they would have stared at my pink towels, my crocks of dried weeds: so much for effect. Of course what would have astonished them most of all would have been my duplications: a city freezer and a country one, two enormous refrigerators, and enough food to feed a small army.

It was one of the things our little band never discussed—our duplications. We all kept egg cartons, and mashed gallon milk containers to start our fires, we all reprimanded our children for eating junk and kept odd dried bits of leftovers in our refrigerator; but the duplications, the double lives which seemed to include doubles of people as well as provender, doubles of husbands, doubles of children, doubles, even, of lovers—that would have shamed us beyond explanation and so we made do with our savings. I remembered how angry Flora had been with me once when I had poured the bacon grease down the drain.

I put on a tight pink shirt—I enjoyed showing my nipples—and a clean pair of bluejeans. Anything else would have looked planned, which in our circle would have signified frivolity. We were all serious people, after all, the women perhaps more so than the men.

Downstairs, there was a crash and Jeff came screaming up. I pushed him away when he burrowed into my thigh. Threatening him with being left behind, I started for the stairs. The threat frightened me a good deal more than it frightened him; I was terrified of delay as though the party was dissolving in front of me. At my heels, Jeff launched into an endless explanation. Injustices, injustices; I have never been able to explain them to my children and their number was always legion. It did not matter, now. I was armed with expectation—eventually, his tears would stop—because I was going, with the children for excuse, to spend the rest of the day with grownups. There would be plenty to eat and drink, a bonfire lighted later, and the promise, the miraculous promise of intimacy.

We were cheery in the car; David did not even make the children fasten their seatbelts. He drove a mile or two above the speed limit, which surprised me. Usually he drove with dazzling caution, noticing wetness or ice on the road which I could never see. Now he was at his ease, the fingers of one hand resting idly on the wheel. It was unlike him, but I did not mind. Sinking into my delicious euphoria, into the cottony layers of expectation, I looked out the window. The landscape seemed formed for my delight. Old fields sloped up from the road to barns and white frame houses. There were sheep in one pasture and a special set of trapezoid barns which we had always admired.

We turned onto the lumpy tree-hung side road. The children cheered. They shouted at their father to speed up over the big bump in the road, but David slowed down, and began to explain to them about the car springs. We passed quietly over the bump without losing the pits of our stomachs. I remembered sailing over it in Edwin's car, years before, with his children shrieking on the roof. They were quite small then and I was startled by Edwin's nonchalance. My own three were safely strapped into our car with David. "Do you think they will hold on to the luggage rack?" I asked Edwin politely, and he laughed, showing me his eyeteeth. "Perhaps we'll be lucky and lose one or two." He was able to say that sort of thing because he never appeared to be burdened by his children; he simply included them in his life. They went with him everywhere. I had often seen them monkeying in the supermarket, shattering crackers in the luncheonette or making a mild disturbance in the movies, with Edwin in the lead, smiling, shedding his charm to cover their dishevelment.

We turned into the little gravel drive, passing the trashcan on wheels which Peter, their eldest, was responsible for wheeling out every morning. In spite of their exuberance in public, the Field children were well-trained. Edwin and Flora did not seem troubled by the uncertainty which dissolved my rules as soon as I made them. I was still torn between the wish to do everything for my children and the conviction that they should at last begin to grow up. Edwin and Flora, I thought, had produced a set of small grownups, with good senses of responsibility and of glee; it seemed as fine a recipe for raising children as any I could imagine.

The Fields' little white house looked neat and bright inside its border of geraniums. Edwin had laid the brick terrace himself, three summers before. That was the first time I saw him without his shirt and I remembered being surprised that a man with so little hair on his chest could look so male, his muscles long and smooth under his glittering wet skin. I had lived my life in the midst of appearances, clothes jerked around on hangers, men who were stuffed, and so Edwin's bare chest had seemed a statement of intent, a flashing intimacy. Of course nothing had happened then. Jeff was a hectic five-year old and I was drained and preoccupied. Two years later, when Jeff was in school all day, I found Edwin's bare chest stored carefully among my fantasies—there were very few—waiting for the ripe time.

There was no one in sight as we drove up to the house except for the dog, a dismal yellow mongrel which everyone hated except for Frank, the second son, who slept with Porky on his chest. Edwin, who had to walk Porky in the city every morning, had once called him the ultimate pleasure, which had sprouted my hope that he and Flora had stopped sleeping together; that hope had been replaced by the fear that he used the dog, instead. Although we had visited the house at least three hundred times, Porky began to snarl at us, and when Jeff reached out to pat him, the dog snapped. David avoided the source of conflict and led us all safely into the house.

A great pot of spaghetti sauce was popping away on the stove; dishes and clothes lay everywhere. As always, the people had vanished. I called, and they appeared, emerging from the cellar, the bathroom, pounding down the stairs; Frank stepped out of the coat closet and smiled with his father's mystery when I asked him why he had been hiding. Flora, her hair flying, dabbed my cheek with a kiss, brushed my forearm with her muscular breast and turned away to stir the spaghetti sauce.

I looked for Edwin, sorting through the milling shapes. He was there, but he passed me quickly without a look or a smile, heading for the telephone. Sometimes when we met, he lifted me up in his arms; other times, he did not seem to see me. I was never sure of the difference, although I was sure of the hurt. Now I quickly reassembled myself—it was important not to show Edwin any sign of pique or pain—while he began to dial.

The children stormed outside and Flora and David sat down to their ritual cup of coffee. They had an odd friendship, foreclosed, narrow and permanent. They began their standard dialogue, touching humorously on their difficulties as the responsible adults in their families; Flora's condescension, as always, annoyed me. Meanwhile, Edwin was talking on the telephone, his back turned to me as he leaned against the wall. The call was long, detailed and yet perfunctory—I was grateful for that—dealing, I finally realized, with a repair he was having made to his car.

Watching me watch him, Flora asked me if I would like a cup of coffee and smiled tenderly at my guilty start and refusal. Standing in the middle of the kitchen, I knew that I was upholding all their expectations; I was the child who had drawn the short straw, who had to be "it." "Aren't you at all attracted to Edwin?" Flora had asked me curiously, over the years; she had watched us together, before we were lovers, with her faint anticipatory smile, planning, imagining the day. Her triumph, which I was just beginning to recognize, took the edge off mine. It was beginning to be clear to me that I was the last of Flora's country friends to draw the short straw.

Flora had remarked several times that fall that she knew I had "a thing" for Edwin; she seemed to find it amusing, as though I had finally revealed myself to be as foolish as she had always surmised. My authority and independence were gone, cancelled by "the thing," and she had even begun to advise me about my children, reminding me to take them to have their shots, handing out aspirin as though I would not have any at home. David seemed to enjoy the situation too. "I have a tiger by the tail," he observed once when I had spent the evening dancing with Edwin. At times, I grew tired of pleasing them and remembered my role in school: bright, stiff-necked, spoiled, I had been the clown who could be counted on to say anything, do anything, and of course, to scream and cry when I was punished.

Finally Edwin hung up the receiver and said, "How are you," without looking at me so that I was not quite sure who he meant. Then in one stride he came and took me in his arms—those long arms, the wrists as narrow as mine. He pressed me confidently, knowing that I would never lean back or wriggle away; I leaned against him for a moment. "A real kiss," he said and I tipped my head back; his lips brushed mine. He smelled as neutral as water, having a great love of baths. After fucking, he would plunge into a hot bath and scrub every inch; he liked me to sit in the water with him. When he had finished washing, he would lie back and talk, the faucet dripping on his shoulder, and I listened with the greatest care, as close to his hidden spontaneity, his secret wishes as I would ever be. I hoped then, in the water, for illumination, for the final breaking of the code. Out of the water, Edwin talked in short bursts and enigmatic phrases which, between ignorance and wishfulness, I could not decipher, yet it was our secret language, shared with no one else. Like a primitive, Edwin used a code so rich in what was omitted that it constantly fascinated me with surmise.

He lifted me off my feet and swung me around, our silently-accepted substitute for the orgasms he wouldn't let me have. "If only we had more time!" I used to plead, as though it would all work if we had hours to play; it did not occur to me then that lack of time was not our only problem. Of course Edwin did not have time to give; I had to be sandwiched between appointments. Now, for an instant, he swung me off the ground and I felt as light and helpless, as exuberant as a child. Then he set me on my feet and disappeared down the steps to the cellar.

Indian giver, I thought.

"Now have a cup of coffee," Flora advised. I wondered how much I was saving her: we were sisters under the yoke. Sometimes at night, I ground my teeth until my jaws ached, at that thought. At other times, our union called up terrifying fantasies: Flora's nipple stoppering my mouth while Edwin fucked me, Flora's mouth on my neglected clitoris. That image was more than I could bear, even in the far reaches of sleep, and I would wake up, sweating. Now I sat down and accepted her cup of coffee.

Flora pushed the gritty sugar bowl in my direction; it was crusted because her children, starved, sometimes ate out of it with their hands. She looked at me with kindness. "Tell me, before Helena and Charles come, how do you think they're getting along?" If I had been a little younger, she would have distracted me, instead, with a good smack.

I was careful, because I knew her code: she would think I was talking about my own marriage. "I think they've gotten everything straightened out. Apparently Charles has started seeing an analyst and it's really working."

"Edwin told me you said analysis is just another form of exploitation."

I was careful not to let her see the hurt. Edwin was not supposed to repeat our conversations. "I was only arguing that ideally treatment should be free."

"Then the patient wouldn't respect it. You know what you get for free is useless, without any value—a handout."

"Paying doesn't mean that much to me."

"You can afford that attitude."

Swiftly, I shifted: money was a dangerous subject. "Generally, I guess I don't have much faith in doctors."

"Since when have you been so disillusioned?" There was a smile like a point of ice in her eyes.

"Since Jeff was born," I answered rapidly. "The obstetrician—you know I switched, on purpose—insisted on forceps—"

Edwin emerged suddenly from the cellar and I lost the last half of what I had meant to say.

"I've never claimed to do anything more than replace neurotic misery with ordinary unhappiness," he said.

"That's saying a lot, even if it is misquoted," I grumbled, annoyed because his mere reappearance had robbed me of what I had intended to say. The births of my children had been turning points, for me; it was all lost in the good-humored grey glance he gave me.

David, making his way into the conversation, asked, "Who else do we have, after all, for help?" I could hear my own opinions caught like flies in the wax of his voice; he was never quite up-to-date. "We can't turn to priests anymore, or parents. Who do we have for trouble except doctors?"

"We might do better with nothing," I said, refusing him the right to compliment my lover who was not after all my cure.

"There are a lot of other things to turn to," Edwin said. "Liquor, drugs, sex." He grinned. "I'm hardly the only opiate of the people."

"Charles told me last July they were thinking of a separation," Flora said, turning us off the track. "I told him I thought it might be a good idea. They ought to think things over."

"We had them over here afterwards to talk," Edwin observed. "They were hardly speaking to each other, at that point, but I think we got them started again."

"Perhaps they are saved, then," I said.

Edwin went on, "I used to think those two held each other up. Now I think they make it safe to fall apart." Before I could answer, he went to the telephone and began to dial;

watching his finger feeling for each hole, I remembered how he felt for me, like a blind man, his fingers hardly discriminating between nipples and buttonholes. I loved his blind fingers. It was only afterwards when the talk began that he discredited what he did so well by instinct, because it was by instinct and not by love or will.

I strained again to hear his cautious conversation, cupped into the telephone. Flora and David had begun to talk about schools—this was the area of Flora's expertise. She knew, each week, which of the city private schools had reached its apex and which was beginning to slide down the other side. She was talking intensely about one which had begun the downward slide, and as she leaned towards David, convincing him, I imagined how the mothers must listen, overawed, as she introduced them to the system.

"I think five o'clock should suit," Edwin said into the telephone, and I lost track of the rest of Flora's monologue as I tried to hear what Edwin was planning. His neat life was full of holes, gnawed by my suspicion. He had been faithful to me for the first six months of our affair (a word which neither of us used, out of moral conviction or the fear of the end)—except, of course, for Flora, the companion of all our dreams. Then, at a party, he had begun to work on my cousin, flattering her, smiling at her, asking her directly what she liked in bed until she was melting in his hands. I don't think he ever saw her again—that would have been intentional—but it did not much matter; he had showed me that he wanted his effects back. I knew that he had reached the limit of his commitment to me and would begin, out of guilt and despair, methodically to destroy it. I knew, for a whole day, and then forgot: it was too painful. I needed my little bite of pleasure, I needed perhaps even more the flimsy everfailing conviction that I was special to him, that my hole or my mouth, my words or my tenderness were creating a lover as they seemed, by their use, to have created me. Now I succeeded in distracting myself from Edwin's telephone conversation by getting myself a slice of bread from Flora's loaded refrigerator; the sight of all that food reminded me of the children, the meals, the planning, the solidity of their life, backed up protectively behind our little life together. I buttered the bread slowly and ate it.

Flora was telling David about her concern for Helena's children if the marriage, in spite of talking, should fail. "Sheila is impossible as it is. So rude. Helena simply ignores it, she lets the child get away with anything. I told her the last time she came here she couldn't eat with her hands at my table, not at her age, she's practically nine years old. Helena of course wouldn't say a word, though she thanked me afterwards."

"Maybe that's why Charles is bored," I said.

"What?" They both turned to look at me.

"Maybe like a five-year-old, he keeps hoping she'll set him some limits. When he was off with that girl—what was her name?—at Mary's last party, he came in looking like a bad child who wanted to be whipped."

"Helena just turned her head away," Flora said thoughtfully. "I thought at the time it was a mistake."

"Resignation is boring, though, at least when you're looking for something else."

"Reaction." She eyed me. "I think you have told me something quite perceptive."

"Use it, next time you get them talking."

David intervened smoothly. "I don't believe they talk to anyone outside, anymore. Flora and I just wanted to get them started."

Flora nodded. I looked at the two of them, fellow conspirators over the coffee cups. "Let's hope they're not two hours late, this time," Flora said, glancing at the clock. "I'd like to get lunch over with."

Edwin changed positions and leaned against the wall, listening intently to whoever was talking to him on the telephone. Pricked, I asked Flora, "Do his patients often call him on the weekend?"

She smiled. "That's one of the questions I never ask, Ann."

David observed, apropos of nothing, "It seems as though this fall everyone is breaking up."

# 3

Tom is knocking at the kitchen door. I can see him through the window, his head turned away to preserve my privacy. I slide my feet into my shoes and go to let him in. He glances at me before asking, "What about setting the tent up in front of the house? People would see it from the road."

"All right."

He turns away, beckoning to his partner, Fred Shingle, a small surly-looking man who hangs around the newspaper store in the village. "You know Fred," Tom tells me.

"Yes. Good morning."

Fred ducks his head.

"We'll set it up in front of the house, then," Tom says, turning away. He is a short man with a large belly swinging out over his belt. His gouged monkey's face is sad and mean. This house belonged to his family for three generations; I have a snapshot of Tom and his brother as children eating watermelon on the side porch. Tom was not particularly pleased to sell us the place and he is not particularly disappointed that we are leaving. We are a strange breed to him, living according to rules which have nothing to do, as far as he can see, with seasonal changes or economic survival.

"We'll get the tent set up and then we'll start moving things out," he says to me, over his shoulder. "Good warm day, they'll be coming in crowds." He is an authentic country man as he gauges the sky. Yet Mrs. T. told me he was a failure as a farmer, sitting drunk in the kitchen all day.

Jeff is standing behind me, so close I nearly fall over him as I turn around. "Are you going to sell my bed?" he asks, for the tenth time. He looks sleepy and cross, having just arisen from that bed which I am selling out from under him; his pajama bottoms hang on his hips, below his navel. He has my body, lean and tense, and I wonder if he will ever be strong or if he will have to settle, as I have, for a certain degree of flexibility.

"We've been over this, Jeff," I tell him patiently. "You know the rule. You can each keep one piece of furniture from your room, in addition to your toys. You didn't choose your bed."

"I'm too big for that damn rocking horse!"

"Do you want to change your mind?"

Without answering, he edges towards the kitchen table and begins to shuffle through the cereal boxes.

"You'll have to decide in the next few minutes," I tell him. "Tom and Fred are putting up the tent and then they're going to begin to empty the house."

Jeff leaves the cereal and runs to the living room window. Over his shoulder, I see Tom squatting by an enormous bundle of canvas. "Is that the tent?" Jeff asks, and his voice and his face change, becoming animated, hopeful.

"Yes, that's the tent." I am as proud as if I stitched it up myself.

"It's going to be a really big one," he says. I kiss the back of his neck, where his thin bond hair lies like tiny feelers on his pale skin; he smells babyish there still, powdery. He is going to allow himself to be drawn into the spirit of the occasion.

It is this, I think, that David finds so hard to accept. If the auction were held in a spirit of defeat, of humble acceptance of life's blows, he might be able to tolerate it. It is the possible springing of hope out of destruction which he finds obscene. Last night, when the children and I were running around the house, slapping red tags on the things we wanted to keep, it was, for a while, a game (until we came to their rooms, at least.) David, standing in the middle of the hall, watched our foolish careening as though he couldn't believe his eyes. Although he told me I could do as I pleased, he had not planned on seeing me enjoy myself.

He has taken a few things for himself—his clothes, of course, and a collection of books and prints. He was supposed to take more, to furnish his own apartment, and I was sorry when he did not arrange for a moving truck to arrive, because whenever David fails to make an arrangement, he is making a point instead. I am not sure, now, whether or not David can interpret this auction, or my enjoyment of it, as evidence of my instability. I do not have much faith in the yellow pad. In order to use it, David would have to place himself in a posture of defiance, even of rage; he would have to agree with himself to use the notes as ammuntion; he would have to think of himself as a man capable of hate.

Outside the window, Tom and Fred are crouching and darting, dealing with a maze of ropes; Jeff, fascinated by their expertise, watches with his nose against the glass. I go back to the kitchen and pour myself another cup of coffee.

When I turn away from the stove, Keith is standing by the table, eyeing the boxes of cereal. "Cereal, again," he complains, not looking at me. "At least I hope you remembered to get some bananas."

"There's one on the bottom shelf of the refrigerator, but it's brown."

Keith sighs, abandoning breakfast, and drops into a kitchen chair: thirteen years old, already in despair. His pajamas gape at the waist, showing his fat white middle. "You always used to cook real breakfasts, eggs, and all, before."

"That's because Daddy was cooking real breakfasts, every other morning. I had to keep up. He would cook sausages, I would cook bacon, or vice versa; I've forgotten. We argued once about which took the most time."

"Where is Daddy?"

"In the guest room, getting dressed." I do not allow myself to remind Keith that this process always takes a while.

He looks towards the door to the porch; he is shifting his eyes regularly around the room to avoid looking at me. "Daddy asked me to go down to the Caribbean with him at Christmas. He's going sailing on Uncle Sheldon's yacht."

I will not show my surprise. Calmly, I remark, "Sheldon always did prefer your father to me. I suppose it's natural. You can't very well have sibling rivalry with your brother-in-law, and Sheldon really did hate me when we were little."

"It's either that or sitting around in New York for three weeks."

"If you're going to eat, eat; I want to clear the table."

"I'm not going to eat. You're in a foul mood, aren't you?" When I do not answer, he goes on, "New York at Christmas really stinks. It rains, and you're always in a bad mood, and there's nothing to do."

"I can't afford to take you to the Caribbean. Grandpa's money that we lived on all these years is nearly gone. Two houses, three children and a husband used it up."

It is not the first time he has heard this and it is not the first time he has refused to believe me. "I guess I'll go with Dad and Uncle Sheldon."

"Have a good trip," I say.

For the first time, he glances at me, and I see the wretched torn boy beneath his arrogance. "It's all right, Keith; I expect you'll enjoy yourself. I want you to enjoy yourself; I'm just angry because the money's gone and it wasn't only me who spent it. You don't want to hear that and I won't say anymore for a while. Talk to your father about it. You'll have plenty of chances, once you're living with him."

"He told me he'll have his place fixed up in another couple of weeks. Can I take my stereo?"

"Of course. It's yours."

The collaboration between my husband and my eldest son sticks like a splinter of bone in my throat. I carry my rattling coffee cup and saucer into the parlor. It is important not to burden Keith with any more guilt. Yet when I think of him sitting in the evenings with his father, sharing confidences, I am ready to die of rage. This is the child I bore and nursed and raised when David was so busy he never even met the pediatrician, so fastidious he could not bring himself to change a pair of diapers, so clumsy that when he tried, once, to feed Keith his strained apricots, he upset the little jar into the lap of his pin-striped suit. And now they are united, and solid, against me: two males. It is the tie that binds.

Until the separation, they were tied by distrust: Keith after all had edged David out of my attention. A baby is so much more satisfying than a dry man. Keith was a hungry angry baby who kept me up night and day with his shrieks, his kicking, his active, changing pace; he was a racer from the start, and he kept me to the mark—with him I reached, for the first time, the limit of my endurance. David watched this from the sidelines, intrigued, perhaps—it was another tiger, of a sort, to be held rather gingerly by the tail.

Now they are united against the common foe. I remember their voices late at night, after I have gone to bed: they sit by the fire with their glasses of crème de menthe and their well-documented injuries. David told Keith, long ago, about Edwin, and my son was devastated. "Peter and I used to be friends," he told me with tears in his eyes. After that, he began to turn his face away from me. His moon-look of devotion and patience, which I depended on without even knowing it, has almost entirely disappeared.

"I don't want to live with you without Daddy," He told me, dryly, finally, when I was discussing our separation. "I don't want to live with you without a man." He imagined, I suppose, an adolescence devoted to making drinks for my friends and taking me to the movies. He is going to live with his father, instead, where he hopes to be free of demands and disillusionment. For a moment, standing in the sunny parlor, I am frightened by my willingness to let him go; I am letting everything go: where will I draw the line? Then I remind myself that it is because my other two, my babies, will still be with me: I can afford to lose one limb.

Molly comes running into the parlor, her face flushed and strained. "The Fields are here! I saw their car!"

David is behind her. "It can't be," he says and goes to the porch to have a look. I stand rooted in the middle of the floor. My heart is pounding: the cliché, like so many others, is revitalized. I thought they might see the announcement of the auction in the local paper, but it never occurred to me that they would come.

David comes back. "It's true," he says. He has turned pale, and for the first time, I am sorry for him.

For his sake, I call back my sangfroid like a genie escaped from a bottle. David is watching me closely. "They're welcome to come," I say. "After all, it's a public event." I have not realized until I say those words how much I want to see Edwin.

"I wonder what they want?"

I do not answer, unwilling to be drawn in, although my curiosity hurts like heartache. We have spent a great deal of time analyzing Edwin's and Flora's motives—assuming that their motives are separate—and that effort took the place of analyzing our own. After all, we have in this situation two pimps and two wreakers: those lines of comparison might have been worth drawing. Instead, we attempted to make of the Fields a common enemy, to unite, briefly, against them; but that was not possible for me. I remembered, after a while, how Edwin feels, and that disrupted the common cause.

"What are we going to do?" David asks.

"We are going to behave as though nothing has happened. Don't frighten the children. There is nothing else we can do." For the last time, I am asking him to be a fellow conspirator, and he seems to agree. When Molly comes rushing back with fthe latest bulletin, we both greet her with an appearance of disinterest; I repeat to her that the auction is, after all, a public event. Deflated, she sits down at the desk and begins to draw a series of large faces on a pad. "I wanted to help with the auction," she complains, swiftly shifting ground. "You promised to wake me up early so I could help and then you forgot."

"There really isn't much more for anyone to do, Molly. You helped me tag the things we want to keep. Tom and Fred are going to take the furniture out; maybe you can help with that."

She looks around the parlor. "In this whole room, we're only keeping that ugly lamp."

It is made from deer's hoof, brittle with age. "That was in your grandfather's lodge in the Adirondacks. I was always fond of it."

"It's ugly," she says. "Why aren't you going to keep this desk?"

David sits down and opens his newspaper; behind it, he will listen to our conversation.

"That desk is too small to be practical," I repeat wearily. "I need a big desk, for paying bills."

"But it's so pretty!" She lifts one of the little brass pulls and lets it fall with a jingle.

"I know, and I remember how you used to enjoy sitting on my lap and opening and shutting all those little drawers. But there won't be room for two desks in our new apartment."

"It sounds like a stinky little place."

"It's all we can afford. I'll take you next week to see it. It's bright, it's full of sun, your room has a bookshelf."

Keith has come in, chewing on a piece of raisin toast. "I thought that desk belonged to your grandmother."

"It did. It came up with all the other things from Washington, when she died. This desk was always in the corner of her bedroom. She kept flowers on it and a photograph of her first husband—not your great-grandfather, he came too late to be admired. The desk was a kind of shrine. She never actually used it. She sat up in bed with a tray on her lap to write her letters."

"Why isn't Daddy taking more stuff?"

"Ask him."

We all look at the newspaper; slowly, it shifts, and David's calm face appears. "What is it?"

I motion to Keith to repeat his question, but his mouth is conveniently full of raisin toast and he simply stares. "I told your father weeks ago he could take anything he wanted, but he never could get a moving truck here," I say.

"Why can't he just keep the things he wants here?"

"Because the new people are going to move in." My voice is crusty, dry; I am so tired of explaining, tired of my own righteousness. Where is the soft woman Edwin used to take in his arms?

"Well, nobody is going to sell my things," Keith announces.

"You've told me that, many times, and I've told you it simply can't be. Now we haven't been through your room together and nothing is sorted out, but you're simply going to have to make your mind up to let the furniture go. The house has to be cleared out. Your father and I agreed on that. We can't take all your junk to the city; there wouldn't be room for it there." As I pile argument on argument, I begin to lose my patience. Turning way, I knock my shin on the rocker. I lean down to rub the bump. "Now get dressed, both of you. It's nearly time for the auction to begin. You may want to go outside when the people have all come."

"I'm not going out there," Keith says.

"Why not?"

He does not answer, and I know he means to guard the door to his room.

"He says it's too embarrassing," Molly explains.

"It is," Keith says. "We're getting rid of everything we own."

"I've told you over and over, I'm sick of telling you—we have to have the cash to live on."

"I can't bear the idea of everybody picking over—" Suddenly he is crying, furiously beating me off with his hands when I try to comfort him.

"Keith," David says, lowering the paper. "It will be all right, son." He adds, to me, "This is all very upsetting."

"Of course it's very upsetting. And it's going to get worse. We are going to have to clear out Keith's room." At that, the boy breaks away from me and dashes up the stirs; I hear his door slam behind him. "There isn't going to be any way around this one," I tell David.

Looking at his calm face, his benevolent soft brown eyes which match his corduroy country suit, I am frightened by the extent of my own power. Pushing against David has always been like pushing against cream, or foam; I am left with the desolating awareness of my own strength. Normal assertiveness begins to seem, in his presence, like the high-pitched barking of an hysterical dog, leg-chained to a lamp-post. I begin to falter. "I need you to persuade him, David. We really have to get his room cleared out."

He lays the newspaper aside; on his lap, I see the yellow pad. "That's not all there is to it. There's your theory, as well."

Molly glances up from her drawing, scenting a confrontation. We both look at her, wish her away, and then settle for her presence as a potentially useful ally.

"Of course, there's my theory," I admit, cornered. I listen to David's silence for a while. In the next room, Jeff, oblivious, is zooming a metal tank around the floor; upstairs, Keith is guarding his room. It seems to me that they are all waiting, listening for my explanation, and I realize that I have counted on their grudging consent. "You'd better tell me what you're getting at," I tell David.

"I don't believe in your theory that people can start over, fresh, with no pasts."

"Neither do I. That's ridiculous. That's not my theory at all. I'll never be able to shed my past, even if I wanted to. I'm keeping that loveseat because I used to sit there while my grandmother told me stories about all the terrible things that can happen to women in this world, but even if I didn't keep the loveseat, I'd hear her voice in my ears every time I go down to the subway. The most I can do is just to change my way of life, and that's hard enough—change what I eat, what I wear, how I spend my time, the rooms I live in. Maybe eventually rearrange things so I can go outside in good weather and stay inside in bad, be with people I like or be alone. But that's ambitious. All I'm trying to do now is just change the look of the rooms where I'm going to live." David glances at Molly. "Is that ridiculous?" I ask.

David looks at his yellow pad, touches a line with his finger. "That's not ridiculous. But I'm not sure that's all you're trying to do."

"Anyway, it's too much!" Keith shouts, from the top of the stairs. "It's too much and it's not fair!" Then he stumps off to his room again and ostentatiously slams the door.

"Keith gets to keep everything, it's not fair," Molly whimpers.

I look at my husband. "David, you are going to have to deal with him. It's not fair to expect the other children to give up their furniture when Keith is keeping everything he has."

David looks again at his pad. "I never thought this auction was a good idea. Too disrupting for them—I told you that."

"But their life is already disrupted, since we separated. I don't see how keeping things is going to heal the split."

"Things mean a lot to them."

"They mean a lot to you." Hastily, I add, "Besides, you agreed with me, two months ago; you agreed to this sale."

"On top of everything else, to expect the children to give up all their things—"

"They're keeping their toys!"

"Well, to give up even their beds—"

"But we agreed, we agreed to this, two months ago."

"I'm sorry, I don't remember agreeing to help you with this. It was all your idea. I told you to go ahead and try. But I warned you it wouldn't work, the children wouldn't stand it. You were determined, there was nothing I could say. But I'm not going to bail you out at the last minute, when it all starts to go wrong."

"It's not all starting to go wrong. The men are here, the tent is here, we're all ready to start. It's just Keith. But you are going to have to help me with Keith. You are not going to be able to sabotage it all." My power, or the illusion of my power, has drained away, leaving me watery. I go into the living room to escape their complicity—Keith and David, Molly and David, each couple united against me. I look down at Jeff, still busily running his tank across the floor. Thank God there is one extra for my side. As I watch him, the sun is abuptly cut off and I turn to the window to see a straining patch of canvas slowly moving across the panes. While we were arguing, Fred and Tom have been putting up the tent. My helplessness vanishes: the tent is going up.

Molly has followed me into the living room. "Look, the tent is going up!" I exclaim. She glances at it perfunctorily. Jeff raises his head and stares, then darts to the window.

"It's going to be really big!" he says.

Molly begins, again, at my elbow. "I want to keep my cradle. It's not fair. Keith gets to keep everything in his room."

"Keith is not going to keep everything in his room. Now go up and get dressed."

"Daddy says I should get to keep my cradle, he says it's an antique."

"Daddy and I agreed on a set of rules," I tell her. "We agreed two months ago, but now he wants to forget that. Each of you chilren was going to be able to keep one big thing." Before she can begin again, I lean down and put my arms around her. "I'm sorry, Molly."

She stands distrustfully within the circle of my arms, her body thin as a stalk of celery. After a while, she begins to mutter, "It's not fair, it's not fair. We used to have a good time and now we don't ever have a good time anymore."

"We do have a good time, still." I sift my memory for examples. "We went to the Bronx Zoo, that day—"

"It's not the same," she interrupts, and I do not contradict her. Of course it is not the same. The magic circle is broken. I hold her for as long as she will allow it and then I let her go. The suffering of children arouses such terrible guilt in us, we adults who are responsible for them; I must cling with all my strength to my faith that my happiness is worth as much as theirs. It is an evil faith.

David comes into the living room, behind me; I catch a whiff of his shaving lotion, which makes me gag. He puts his pad on the children's working table and, leaning down, he begins for the first time to write. I am overwhelmed by the sight of his small hand moving slowly along the lines. "If you are going to stay in this house, you can't just be a spy," I tell him. "You are going to have to do something about Keith."

He does not stop writing. "You didn't make that a condition when you invited me."

"I was too upset, at the time."

He glances up at me with a little smile. "I'm here, Ann, because you invited me, which was only correct since I own half these things. But I am not here to help you. The auction was not my idea. You never even bothered to discuss it with me until you had made up your mind. None of this was my idea." He sounds as though he is looking over a vast plain where my ideas are marching, a disorderly throng.

"But the other children will be completely demoralized if Keith gets away with this."

"Gets away with what?" Jeff asks softly from the window.

"Please go out of here, Jeff." But he stays glued.

"You should have thought of that before," David tells me.

"I thought the children agreed with me. They seemed to agree with me, in the beginning. What were you and Keith talking about, last night?"

"His school."

"I don't believe it—" I am no longer sure of my own doubts and fears, yet I have to give them their normal, ordinary weight.

David shrugs and looks away.

"What do you want," I say. It is not and has never been a question. David wants only what he is given; at this moment, he wants nothing. Yet he will be revenged for his own compliance.

"The tent's up," Jeff announces, at the window.

"You are going to help me with Keith," I tell David.

David looks down at his pad and corrects a word.

"What are you writing there?" I shriek.

"Mommy, don't scream like that!" Jeff is suddenly beside me, pulling at my arm. David tucks the pad quickly away.

"Just some notes."

"My God, I can't stand it." I clutch my hair with my hands.

"I'll get you a cup of coffee," David says. We look at each other. Hatred, so much more nourishing than love, is briefly illuminating his face. I know that I am looking flushed and vital, too, rage speeding fresh blood through my veins. The energy with which we are trying to hurt each other was never available for loving.

"It's all right," I say, patting Jeff's shoulder and at the same time trying to put him a slight distance off. "Don't worry." He goes back to his window.

Waiting for my coffee, I remember the years whe David and I were gentle and kind to each other, offering tidbits of comfort and understanding, adjusting a pillow, pouring a cup, united by our distrust of common reality. That was when the fucking began to stop. Two invalids must spare each other. Instead, we lay side by side in bed, chastely, companionably, like two children sharing a fear of the dark.

It was better that way. The disappointment otherwise was too much for either of us to bear. David had stopped coming with me—he blamed his allergy medicine—and I had never come with him, even in the beginning when everything seemed possible.

For years, I prevented myself from understanding or plumbing my own emptiness, the void I pitched into when David pulled out. I cooked and bought and made babies, instead, filling up the gaps, and of course, I read. Eventually I stumbled on an article in a woman's magazine which convinced me that there was a cause for the despair which gnawed me after David was gone. I told him in a French restaurant that I had never had an orgasm, either with him or with anybody else. It was wine-choosing time (or whine-choosing time, as Edwin, my punmaker, would say) and David looked up from the list. "I'm so sorry to hear that," he said gently, with mild surprise. He comforted me then as he had for other disappointments, with a soft pat on my shoulder, with affection, with the unspoken object lesson of his own resignation: we had both run dry. The magazine, I told him, advised women like me (I had never belonged to a group before) to try a vibrator. That made sense to David, and he bought me one, the following week, shielding me from the embarrassment of having to buy one for myself. It sat on the bedside table in its cheap box, a plastic wand I filled with two D-cell batteries; when I turned it on, it buzzed away like Jeff's tin tank. I was embarrassed by the thing and half-afraid of it. Finally one night, when David was in the city, I tried it. It gave me a spasm as intense as the convulsion that sometimes precedes death, a revelation which should never have come to me so cheaply and so fast. Fascinated, I tried the device again and again, hurrying the children into bed in the evening so that I could experiment; there was pleasure hidden in that spasm, and relief, once I had overcome my fear of pain. After a while, the device seemed to lose its magic, and the spasms did not come without ditchdigging work and fantasies which horrified me. I no longer had the warmth of David's body, pumping away vaguely above me, for comfort. When I came, I came around emptiness.

That was when the hope began. With Edwin.

"Make it stiff," he told me, a year ago, flopping on the bed in the guestroom. It was the day after Thanksgiving and all our children were playing Monopoly in the parlor; we had locked the door. I knelt over him on the bed, unzipped his fly and took his limp penis in my mouth. The delight of feeling him stiffen as I sucked blotted out, for a moment, the children's voices in the next room. Edwin lay quietly, his hands behind his head, submitting to my ministrations, possibly enjoying them, as I imagined one day he would pleasure me. Then he took me rapidly, pulling off my pants, pressing his penis into my vagina. It was over so quickly. He was half-starved, and I was starving in a different way. As he washed himself in the sink, I pressed my hands between my legs as though to staunch a wound. "I hurt. I'm empty, it's no good for me this way. Get a sitter for the boys tonight so we can have some time together."

He looked at me, alarmed. "But I don't want to get a sitter. The children depend on me to be with them, especially when Flora is away."

"Flora asked me to take care of you when she went back to town."

"You are taking care of me." He smiled, came to the bed, reached down, and touched my hair. It was so rare for him to touch me when we were not fucking that my eyes filled with tears.

"Edwin, I need you—I need more of you than this. I need you to stay inside me."

"I'm sorry," he said quietly, "but this is all there is."

"I just want more of what you have, more time with you, more of the same, not something different," I pleaded.

He turned towards the door, buckling his belt. I went around the other way, through the kitchen, to come into the living room separately. By then, I had adjusted my expression. It seemed to me that I would not be able to outlive my despair and yet of course I went on, fixing the children's lunch, pouring their milk.

In the afternoon, we all went for a walk in the woods, the older children running ahead along the trail that was no longer marked, now that the leaves were off the trees, the younger ones tagging behind, complaining about the cold. Edwin shouted and ran and leaped for low branches, I ran beside him as though running and playing with him would make me whole. To run, to eat, to talk—surely that would take the place of the deep touching he would not give me. "An affectionate relationship is the only thing that keeps two people together," he said later, when we were walking back. "That's what you're trying to build, with me."

"But I don't want an affectionate relationship, if it means just being friends."

He looked at me, startled. In the house, he went at once to the telephone, to call Flora in the city; he discussed this and that with her, his face feral and animated, his eyes fixed on me as I moved around the kitchen, pretending to ignore him. Finallly I went upstairs and choked down a tranquilizer, trying to put a weight on my rage. He must have hung up, at once; he called to me from the bottom of the stairs: "Where are you? Where are you?" mocking his own uneasiness. When I came down, he said, "You see, I won't even allow you to go to the bathroom alone anymore." I wanted that— I wanted his need. It took the place of my own satisfaction.

Later that evening, he took his children home. I woke up in the middle of the night, in my small cold room, in darkness which was like the inside of my own head. I lay awake for a long time, my hands clenched by my sides. He had fucked me in the room next to my children; he had exposed them to my desire. He had forced me to do that because he was not willing to find a time when we could be alone—sex snatched lik an irresistable bit of filth, a moment's wallowing. So rage chooses its own target. I felt stifled, and yet full of life, full of flaming energy. I got out of bed. Dressing, jerking on my boots, I went downstairs and sat at the kitchen table until the sky turned grey beyond the pine trees on the rocky ledge. Then I wrote a note for my children and went out to the car. The windshield was frosted over, the steering wheel so cold I held it with the tips of my fingers. I drove down the two-lane highway between fences beginning to appear out of the dark. There was not a single other car. Chasing my own headlights, I drove as fast as the car would go: eighty, then ninety, till the trees leaped and I was frightened. I slowed down on the little road. I turned into their drive, stopped the car, and walked to the front door. The dog, as always, began to bark. I tried the door; to my horror, it was locked. I had never thought of it being locked, I had imagined that I would open it silently and creep up into their bed. I began to bang on the door with my fists. Then I kicked it with the toes of my leather boots. Finally a light went on inside and I saw Edwin's pale face through the glass panel. He looked frightened, and for a minute I thought he would not open the door.

He opened it.

I pushed inside, pushed against him, snatching his forearms, then his shoulders, holding him with all my strength. "I hate you. I hate you. You treat me like dirt. You fuck me with the children all around. You won't find time for me, you don't care." I snatched his limp hand and bit into the fleshy part of the base of his thumb, biting so deeply I could feel the muscle under the skin and tissue. He did not pull his hand back, did not exclaim. His other hand fell on the back of my neck. I undid my teeth and looked at his hand: it was set with the prints of my incisors. "Edwin. Edwin." I was sobbing, terrified. He took me in his arms, standing rigid, staring over my head at the meadow appearing out of the shadows of the night. Later, he gave me oatmeal, and we sat in silence in the scruffy little kitchen, waiting for the children to wake up. I clung to his hand. He was the only man who had ever let me rage, and like a child with a treasure, I inspected from time to time the blue dents I'd left at the base of his thumb. I knew then I loved him.

# 4.

"You're not breaking up," I said to Flora. We were in her kitchen.

She stared at me. Her brown eyes looked small in her large, rosy, always slightly damp face. When she turned her eyes away, the planes of her face continued to confront me with an appeal I did not want to see. "Edwin and I have our ups and downs. But I don't believe anyone could come between us."

"Of course not. That's not the way it happens."

"It happens that way all the time, to other people. But we have our arrangement. He can do what he wants, on the side." She glanced at Edwin, still caught on the telephone.

"I think I'll go see about the children," David said, tactfully, and made his way out of the kitchen.

"David doesn't like this kind of talk," I said.

"I suppose it embarrasses him."

"Yes: your contract. Or its effects."

She did not respond to my irony. "It works quite well, actually. Edwin has his little pleasures, but they don't intrude on our life together; he wouldn't allow them to."

It was on the tip of my tongue to tell her that Edwin and I had our contract too; Flora's objectivity was catching. Edwin had presented me with his terms before our first night, in the field: "No marriages and no divorces," he had said and I, wanting him, had agreed, too naive to understand exactly what he meant. Later I had begun to wonder about the order of events in his pronouncement: surely divorces should have preceded marriages.

Edwin hung up the telephone and passed us, frowning, his mind on something else. I felt the movement of air along my arm as he passed; it was as close as I could come, at that moment, to touching him. He went down the stairs to the basement.

"Edwin has a funny little smile when he hears your name," Flora said.

"Has he."

She fingered her coffee cup. "I know if there was anything between you, you'd think of me, you wouldn't let it get serious."

After a while, she got up to stir the spaghetti sauce. Looking at her broad back, her servicable haunches, I tried half-heartedly to believe that she loved Edwin and that she would suffer if she lost him. She was entirely lacking in the mannerisms of affection—never touched him, kissed him, smiled at him, teased him or asked after his comfort, and would have scorned all such outward shows as either vulgar or hypocritical. It was easy for me to believe that they used each other only as social commodities, escorts at dinner parties, partners in anxiety and planning. I had always discounted the strength of that kind of bond because I disapproved of it.

Helena came suddenly into the kitchen; I had forgotten her, in the interval since I last heard her name, and now her presence seemed irrelevant, an intrusion. "Can I put some of these things in your fridge?" she asked, her arms full of grocery bags which she dropped on the table before kissing Flora's cheek and then, in the same motion, mine. Without waiting for permission, she began to unpack the bags on the table between us, slamming meat, milk and butter into the refrigerator. Dark, small, lively, she reminded me of a dragonfly as she darted back and forth. In five minutes, it seemed that she had been with us the whole day. "It's so much cheaper to do the whole week's shopping at the A&P," she explained as she saw that we were watching. "We came straight from there and we're going straight from here to the city."

Flora got up to help her.

"How do you keep the frozen things from defrosting in the car?" I asked.

"I never buy frozen things. Not at this time of year, when the fresh produce on the stands is so cheap."

They talked for a bit about prices, a subject I had always been able to ignore. The energy which fueled their cleverness about money went into my dreams, which took up a good deal of my waking life, dreams of a different life, a simple life centered on sexual love. Flora looked at me and laughed. "Look at her, she's off in her daze again."

I got up and took an egg carton to show that I was involved. There was no room for it in the packed refrigerator. "I was thinking about all the telephone calls I'll have to make when we get back to the city Monday," I lied. "They pile up, over the weekend."

"Well, if you insist on doing all your ordering over the telephone . . . Doesn't money matter to you at all?" Flora teased.

"Oh, I like it," I said, to make them laugh.

"Wait till you have to learn fifteen different ways of cooking cabbage," Helena said. "I like the planning part—adding up, keeping count of what I spend—but when I have to come down to dealing with what I've bought . . . Cabbages . . ."

"You should join my co-op," Flora said. "They give us more potatoes than cabbages."

Both women lived on the upper West Side, although they seldom saw each other in the city. Their apartments seemed identical, long rows of brown rooms high above West End Avenue. My pale-yellow co-op on East Eighty-Ninth Street was a devastating piece of frivolity, by comparison.

George, Helena's husband, a short stout man in his early forties, passed rapidly through the kitchen, kissing us all on his way, even his own wife. Flora and I glanced at each other, at that. George went down to the basement where Edwin was starting the electric saw. It squealed like a shot rabbit; Flora grimaced, threw her eyes up and slammed the basement door.

David came in from checking on the children. He kissed Helena affectionately, held her off to admire her face, and then began to help her pile her cans back into the grocery bags. He did not need to be told what Helena was doing because he had a great sensitivity to domestic arrangements and could always be counted on to help. After the bags were packed, David offered to carry them out to the car and Helena, very pleased, followed him.

Flora peered out of the kitchen window, her hand expertly twitching the curtain aside. "Are those two having a thing?"

"I'm afraid not." It was easy for me to imitate her jaunty tone.

"It would be good for David if they did have a thing," Flora observed. "Good for his self-confidence, generally." She began to scrape the breakfast plates, now and then snatching a morsel of bacon or solidified egg and cramming it into her mouth. I had never seen her eat, except at dinner parties or off her children's plates. "You wouldn't mind if they were having a thing, would you?"

"I'd be delighted."

"That's the way I feel. It doesn't mean anything, after all. It doesn't take anything away from me. Why should I object?"

"No reason at all."

This time, she didn't quite believe me. "It's the age, I think," she said quietly. "Forty-five and they still don't have what they want."

"Do they know what they want?"

"Edwin's been trying to finish his book on hyperactive children. He's been trying to finish it for five years. He has the notes and the outline—he finished those last summer when he was alone in the city—but he can't seem to get started on the book."

"He doesn't seem very concerned about it."

"You're right, he's not desperate, he's perfectly comfortable," she said crisply. "It's only boredom that drives him to other women. We call them his fuckees. He never wants to see them again, after it's over. I say to him, 'So-and-so's in town, shall I invite her to dinner?' But he never wants me to."

The constriction around my throat tightened till I could hardly swallow. "He tells you about them?"

"Of course. That's part of our arrangement. He doesn't tell me at first, he waits until he thinks I'm ready."

"And are you?"

"Oh, yes."

"Don't you ever mind, Flora?"

"No, why should I mind? They don't mean anything to him." She loaded the last plate into the dishwasher. I did not try to help, knowing from experience that Flora would wave me aside. "It would be different if they talked—had a relationship."

"Why does he do it," I said, not making it a question because I was terrified by her assurance.

"Oh, he does it for a little adventure, a little excitement."
She began to fill the silverware basket. "It makes our life
together better, actually; especially in bed."

I stood up abruptly. My chair fell over. "I'm going out to
see about the children."

"I'll come with you."

"Don't bother." I went out, knowing she would be too wary
to follow.

I stopped outside, by the door. I looked at the flowerbed
which Edwin had dug last October and filled with chrysanthemums, for Flora—Flora, who did not like flowers and was
embarrassed by the gesture which she did not know how to
repay. I clenched my fists, feeling my own lack of strength in
the delicate imprint of my nails in my palms; I would have
liked to ram them through. Flora, Edwin's mouthpiece,
speaking his truth which I was resisting with every muscle
and every fiber, but also with wishfulness—the child's pale
scream: I will not have it this way because I do not want it
this way. "Kicking against the pricks," my mother called it, a
modest euphemism. I began to summon up the arguments
for my own case, the case for love, untrammeled, arguments
drawn from thirty-eight years of speculation, dream, denial,
drought, of avoiding the awareness of my own needs and the
lengths to which I would go, once aware, to satisfy them.
Sweat ran down the insides of my arms, my shirt was sticking
to my back. It occurred to me that I was not going to be able
to stand this rage. "Get out of this situation," I said, aloud.
"Get out, just get out." The command seemed simple and
yet it had no force; it was a command out of another life.
The past defined but did not explain. When I was seven, my
uncle threw me up in the air, throwing me again and again
and catching me again and again until I seemed to sail, lost,
freed, my body limp as a petal. When Edwin lifted me in his
arms, I flew again. Yet what did the connection mean? And
why was it made now, rather than last year or next year or
never? It still seemed more to the point to remember Edwin's
long smooth body, taking me fast and coming fast in order
to get it over with and then rocking me in his arms, wordless,
starving as I was starved—his precious warmth, in the instant
after orgasm, before the talking began.

I saw my children up at the swings; they seemed very far
away and I could not interpret their dodging and darting,

their cries. Pain, or joy? Edwin's two oldest boys detached themselves and began to throw a ball back and forth, and I wondered what they, edging into adolescence, thought of this thick hot atmosphere. What did they question, what did they conclude? They looked at me now, sideways, curious and wary, with their father's light grey eyes. Perhaps the most terrible consequence of it all was the children's loss of trust. They were fed by our lies, which cancelled their own observations. "I think you like Edwin," Jeff said to me once, long ago, on the way to nursery school. "You kiss him a lot." Frightened, I told him that he was mistaken and he looked up at me, his face clouded.

David and Helena were walking towards me from the car; they were deep in conversation. I called, "What are you talking about?"

"You," Helena said soothingly. ,

"Don't you have anything better?"

"Now, don't get irritated. We've all been concerned about you, this fall—that was what David was telling me. We love you, you know, we all love you, and you seem so hectic."

In spite of myself, I was flattered. She had sensed my essential, my flourishing disorder, from which I had garnered the strength to snatch at what I wanted—to get rid of my cleaning woman, at an hour's notice, with a handful of bills, to strip the bed and make it up with fresh sheets and then to stand by the front door, waiting for Edwin to ring the bell.

"I've been having a good time," I said.

Helena looked at me with intense surmise. "Well, I hope you know what you're getting into, I hope you don't wear yourself out. You look very thin."

"Don't worry," I said.

"She can take care of herself," David said, and went into the house.

"I'm afraid I've offended you," Helena began rapidly to apologize. "I've been so busy this fall, I haven't had time to think—the legal aid, and then Sheila is a handful, right now, she's going through something—I must talk to Edwin about it—she's up at night; I've lost track of my friends. I'm sorry. We must get together in the city and have lunch and a good talk."

Nothing could have been further from what I wanted: no one was going to touch my secret life. "I just saw you last weekend," I reminded her, turning towards the house. "The weekends . . . Somehow they don't seem to count." Still asking for forgiveness, Helena trailed behind me. "David asked me to talk to you, you know; that's the only reason I said anything. He thought you'd find it easier to communicate with a woman friend." She said it ironically, twisting the phrase as we never twisted other hard-used terms—daughter, son, husband, lover. "I promised him I'd try, and now I'm sorry."

"Try what?" Before she could answer, I went on, "How can women be friends or even women-friends as long as they are mouthpieces for men?" Seeing her face, I was ashamed; it was too easy to loose my anger on Helena. "Never mind. I'm in a bad mood—I'm starved: I wish Flora would dish out some food."

Let off, Helena began to clown; she pretended to pull out a pad and pen. "Madam, as the married mother of three children, could you give us your opinion of the nude men currently displayed in the centerfold of a certain woman's magazine?"

I looked at her disdainfully, pressing down a laugh.

Humbled, she confided, "I sometimes think I'm the only woman in this country who isn't turned on by the sight of a dangling penis. I always think of Sylvia Plath: turkey neck and gizzards."

"An erection might be more appealing," I said, grudgingly, remembering how long it had taken me to look at Edwin's penis, that instrument of fear and delight.

"I don't know . . ." She seemed about to make an unwarranted confession.

"Did you enjoy the party, last weekend?" I asked quickly.

"Don't avoid me," she pleaded. "I was tactless, I guess, but I was just trying to get you and David to talk. Charles and I both feel that once you stop talking—"

"Talking. You all have so much faith in talking."

"Well, words are our only tools."

"If words are our only tools, we're crippled. What about touching? What about tasting, or smelling? Don't you draw any conclusions from that? Have you ever smelled a man when he's afraid?"

"I wouldn't want to," she said, wrinkling her nose.

"You're right, it's a terrible smell. It means you've gone too far. Do you need words, on top of that, to understand?"

"They are our only tools," she repeated.

"If you mean, for power . . ."

Edwin slammed out of the house with the other two men at his heels. He stared at me, suspicious of my closeness to Helena; I stepped back. He had no need of words, to order me. He passed, lugging the orange chain saw. "We're going to cut firewood," David explained. Edwin glanced back—"Come on!"—his eyes animated in his pale face. He looked gleeful, stealing the advantage—taking my husband away up the hill. Charles followed along at the tail like the youngest brother, charitably included. I watched them go; Edwin stalked as though he was wearing a gilt paper crown. "A leader of men," I murmured to Helena, "or at least of women." He had had her, too, three years before, in the back of a Volvo station wagon, a fact I usually tried to forget. "That was the act of a desperate man," Flora had said, when she heard.

Helena, alarmed, went into the house; the screen door, which Edwin had banged, closed behind her with a snuffle. I knew she would tell Flora, in the kitchen, that I was in a bad mood, and they would search out the causes. Later, Flora would reprimand me privately for making Helena feel even more of an outsider, and we would smile at one another, covertly, ashamed of the pride we took in forming the inner circle. Flora and I had been to the same Eastern college, and we could fill out each other's stories with details from debutante parties, heartless families, the petty desperation of boarding school. Helena had grown up in the South and would never share our polish and dash. Tolerated in her small town where Jews were too useful to be ignored (who else, after all, could be counted upon to sit on all the charitable boards and support the annual crusade for children?), Helena made a specialty of her provincialism, exaggerating her accent and her plainness. Flora knew, however, that Helena often felt excluded, snubbed by Charles' law partners and merely tolerated by their wives for whom she cooked "down-home" meals which would have put her mother to shame: cornbread, black-eyed peas—"Nigger food," Helena herself called it, once, sweeping away at one stroke all her attempts to have some authentic color.

The chainsaw began to shriek, at the top of the hill. I looked up in time to see the children running towards their fathers. Working together, they held themselves apart; there would be no accidental touching, no conversation other than jokes. The links between the three men were provided by the women. They had nothing else in common, after five years of shared weekends and holidays, and were as wary of each other as they had been at the beginning, when we had all used the same contractor to refurbish our newly-bought country houses. Then I had thought the men were suspicious of each other because the contractor favored Edwin, giving him lower prices for the same jobs—Edwin always worked with him. The suspicions had not faded when the work was done. As far as I could see, the men never talked to each other, although they shared many hours, many tasks; even when drunk, they did not discuss their jobs, their incomes, their wives or anything else that might pertain. They clung to the fringes—movies, a new book—letting the women toil at the center. David and Charles both said that they admired Edwin, who never talked about himself, never complained. Edwin's pride, like Flora's, held the group together. It had no other natural focus: except for Edwin's games in the underbrush, and I was trying not to think of that.

Watching from my safe distance, I thought there was something ludicrous about the intense way the men were bending over the chainsaw. Even the children saw it, and, impressed, withdrew giggling. Edwin was the only one who was actually handling the machine. Charles and David were both city boys, fast risers from low beginnings, without the country skills which Edwin possessed as though by birthright. They would have been frightened of the chainsaw if Edwin had turned them loose with it. Edwin's ability to tear down, repair and rebuild had less to do with the strength of his arms and back and the delicacy of his manipulating fingers than with the fact that his father had made a good deal of money by patenting a kind of nylon tubing widely used in lawn furniture, and so had been able to buy a house outside Toronto when his son was born—a real farm, equipped with machinery and animals and a farmer who knew how to deal with both. The only baby picture of Edwin I had seen showed him at four or five, grinning as he steered a tractor.

Helena came out of the house, carrying a coffee cup, her conversation with Flora as fresh as a blush on her face. "Flora is so good," she said with a long, quivering sigh. "She never seems to get tired of hearing me complain, and she always gives me such good advice."

"That's why she never has to complain."

"Well, you know, she has her life in shape. She and Edwin know exactly what they want, they know each other's goals, they accept each other." She spoke with the fervor of a convert. "Now that Flora is teaching fulltime, she's become so well-organized. She's pleased about her job and the children are fine. They don't seem to have many problems," Helena finished quickly and pressed on before I could question, "I mean, problems they can't handle. Flora says they talk everything out in the morning, when they take their bath together." She must have seen me wince. "It is amazing, isn't it, that they take their bath together?"

"I don't want to talk about it," I said. She was silent and I realized she was about to offer some ill-timed consolation. "Why are those three men not friends, after all this time?" I asked, gesturing towards the racket on the hill.

"I suppose they're more cautious than we are. They take longer, to get started."

"I don't believe they'll ever get started. They have their chainsaws and their wheelbarrows and their rakes and shovels, though."

"And we have our needlepoint and our pots and pans. And children," Helena reminded me.

"Yes: the children do seem to be ours."

"Except for Edwin's and Flora's. He even takes them to the dentist."

There was a shriek, from the hill; one of the children had been hurt. Helena rushed off. It was Chrissy, screaming by the swing; the heavy seat had crashed into her head. The men were still absorbed in their commotion: not a head turned: and the other children stood staring helplessly. I watched Helena snatch up the big longlegged girl and press her to her breast, covering her with kisses. As she squatted in the grass, holding the child, I decided that the crisis had passed. Even the children were turning away. Yet I could not take my eyes away from the tight knot Helena made, with Chrissy. There was so little contact between the rest of us that the knot looked potent, almost erotic.

"Remember, it's nothing but sex," Edwin had said to me over and over when we fucked, but was it that, or rage, or love, or despair, or nothing at all he felt when he came inside me, silently, his face buried in my neck?

Helena stood up and came towards me, carrying the child, who contently draped on her mother's arms was sucking her thumb. "Is she all right?" I asked.

"Just a little dazed. I'll sit out here with her, for a while." Helena's dignity embarrassed me. As she sat down on the bench, I went inside.

"Just in time," Flora said, when she saw me. "I need you to carry out the food. What were you doing, anyway, lurking out there by yourself?"

"Not much," I admitted. We all avoided spending time alone or even the imputation of spending time alone. "Oh, poor you!" Flora had commiserated when I had stayed a weekend alone in the city, to try to sort things out.

Yes, but, I reminded myself as I was loaded with hotdog rolls, mustard and ketchup, yes, but remember the pale glare of the television set that Saturday night when I lay alone in the huge bed, my insomnia growing larger and more ominous as time passed until it seemed to lie on my chest like an enormous cat, its eyes pressed to mine. Its furry weight crushing out my breath. By three A.M., I was convinced that I would never sleep again without David next to me, his placid touch on the back of my neck, his feet meekly gathered together with mine. Dummy love, I called it, but it had its place. Then I put my hand between my legs and strummed, forcing the orgasm which only the vibrator brought me, until my clitoris was sore and I was crying, betrayed by my own body, the victim of a love that led nowhere, not even to that moment of oblivion, a dependence like a commonplace addiction to candy or cigarettes, spreading year by year across the surface of my life. I began to count the things I had never done with David: never travelled with him or sung with him, fought with him or come with him. It sounded like a popular song. "He's a zero," I said, under my breath, snatching up a tower of paper cups. Saying that shielded me from the thought that if I was not a zero, I was at best a very low number, a one or a two—for the list of things I'd never done alone was even longer. Together, we made a paltry figure.

"Chrissy got hurt by the swing," I said to Flora, to distract myself.

She shoved a bottle of ginger ale into my arms. "I knew something like that would happen. The children are overexcited. Let's hope we won't have to make a trip to the hospital today." She opened the refrigerator. "My God! Look what they've done to my cake!"

One side had been clawed off. "How horrible, maybe it was Sheila," I said.

"No chance, it was one of my dirty boys." She stood staring at the mutilated cake. "I don't know how much longer I'm going to be able to stand them—Saul especially; he's impossible this year. His language! I tell you, it is foul." Reaching in, she began to paste bits of cake and icing into the tear. "I fine him a dollar for each one of these words. He's already run up fifteen dollars this weekend." She took the cake out and slammed it on the counter.

"It doesn't look so bad," I said.

"It's ruined, but I couldn't care less. They can eat it or not, it doesn't matter to me." Turning to the freezer, she opened it and began to snatch out package after package of hot dogs. "I meant to take these out at breakfast but we never had breakfast. Edwin was up at five, tramping around in his boots; he woke me up—I was furious. I didn't wake up again until eleven and by then they were all out in the woods, hunting for pinecones for the bonfire. I forgot all about the damn hot dogs."

I touched them; they were as solid as cartridges. "Maybe they'll thaw out, over the fire."

"All I really wanted to do today was stay in bed."

"You've been very busy." I branched out into sympathy. "I don't know how you manage it all. That long day at school, and now you have the strike to deal with—all those meetings." Guilt gave what I said its shine; Flora began to look mollified. "Have you started to shop for my suit?" she asked shrewdly, seizing the opportunity, and I was ashamed to admit that I had not yet begun. "Oh well, it doesn't matter," she said, dismissing my effort as well as my failure; clothes, after all, like most pleasures, had no immediate reality for

Flora. As I started for the door I brushed against her shoulder and she drew back. Flora never touched anyone, except for a fluttering uncertain pat or her ritual cheek-kiss. Whether she was touched, in the midst of her whirlwind, remained to be seen.

The squeal of the chainsaw stopped and I knew Edwin would be coming down the hill. I rushed out the door, hoping to catch him alone, to taste his voice. I stumbled on the step and nearly dropped my tray, as awkward and eager as a child. The men were already ahead of me, carrying logs down the hill. I ran to catch up, passing Edwin's vegetable garden—his pride—and heading for the clearing at the edge of the woods. Helena was waiting in the clearing, oddly poised, with Chrissy at her side. Edwin crouched down and deposited his armful of logs, the other two men following suit. They seemed to be laying gifts at Helena's feet and she bowed gracefully, accepting. Or perhaps they were preparing to burn her at the stake? I felt as though I was running through water, hurrying clumsily to interrupt the scene. Edwin smiled at Helena. I came up behind them, leaned down, and put my tray on the ground. I was close enough to touch him but he did not look at me. Crouching, he delicately aligned the logs. He was utterly remote from me, justified by the task, and would remain remote for as long as he sensed my need. I had learned never to try to get his attention. Charles asked him, "Do you want the matches?"

"Not yet."

I wished I had something to give.

David began to talk to Helena about the movie which we had all seen in the city the week before. "My wife called it a tour de force," he said, going on to repeat my opinion in full. "What did you think about it?" I asked, with great restraint. I was trying to break David of the habit of quoting me. At dinner parties, I often picked out his voice through the jumble of conversation; he would be relating my latest exploit, with pride and animation. "She simply went and told them at Bloomingdales . . ." At these times, I felt like a trained dog, a poodle walking on its hind legs for its keeper; his image for me was different. "You are an eagle," he had said suddenly, once a few weeks after I had begun to fuck with Edwin; like the others, David stood to profit from my secret life. No one knew what was going on between Edwin and me, no one knew; yet the atmosphere we all lived in, the sea of lies, was warmer by several degrees.

David was already apologizing. "It's just that you express yourself so well. I seem naturally to pick up your opinions."

I said, "What did you think about the movie? I was so busy lecturing you about it, it's no wonder you don't remember what you thought," I added hastily, stricken by his look. Then I explained to Helena, "The movie's about a woman who can only fall in love after she's been turned into a victim. The terrible thing about it is that it's partly true."

"You know you don't believe that," Flora said, coming up behind me with the hot dogs in a basket.

"Ah, but I do," I said. "Down with pride—"

"Female masochism has outlived its usefulness," Edwin said.

We all laughed.

I went on, to him, "It wasn't ridiculous, you know, when she kissed the man's feet."

"Movies are what we live by," Charles interrupted before Edwin could reply. "Sometimes I think the rules we live by are derived entirely from movies, and articles in magazines."

Flora said, "I never read that stuff, I simply don't have the time."

Separating the frozen hot dogs with Edwin's pocket knife, Flora shone with the passionate intensity of all her evasions. She had her own vocabulary, her set of perceptions, and it was not necessary for her to enlarge either one or the other to suit her following. She would be teaching us manners, baking bread and saving money long after we had run through the best books and the best ideas the year had to offer. That she was limited by her stability did not discredit it. She had found a place for each of us, in her hierarchy, and a use which was becoming increasingly plain. Even Edwin has his place, his niche, his celebration as the instrument of Flora's wrongdoing, the marker for her hidden impulses. Hating my own conclusion—too smart, too neat—I looked up the hill at the trees, bathed in warm light.

After a while, I noticed that David was looking crushed. "I'm sorry about the movie," I said.

Edwin looked up at me from his fire. He noticed every change in my voice, more sensitive to my tone than to my expression which he considered planned for effect, like my mascara or my perfume. He was particularly sensitive to the dying echoes of my affection for David, not out of jealousy, which he was not able to feel, but because he wanted to be able to pierce my disillusion when I complained about my husband. "But you enjoyed arguing with him about the train schedule last Saturday," he had reminded me, a week before, to interrupt one of my diatribes. Edwin had a longer view of my life than I could possibly tolerate. He wanted me never to change. Once, in our bath, I had stripped off my wedding ring, and he had stiffened into silent rage. Later, he repeated, several times, with a dull finality, "Never leave your husband. Never leave your husband. Never leave him. I'll never see you again, if . . ." I had not believed him.

# 5.

Time is shortening in front of me: the auction will begin in half an hour. I must do something about Keith. Leaving the others in the living room, I start up the stairs. His door, at the end of the hall, is closed, and when I try the handle, the bolt rattles in its catch. I knock, politely. "Keith, I want to talk to you. Let me in."

He mutters something indistinguishable and does not open the door.

I knock again, too hard, the side of my hand crashing into the wood.

"Let me in! We have to talk, Keith, we can't handle it this way."

He does not answer. In the space of seconds, I am rendered entirely helpless, reduced to a fantasy of splitting the door with an ax. I go to sit down on the blanket chest at the other end of the hall, trying to wait, trying to let my hands rest idly in my lap. I look out over the field, where the housing development will be. A year ago, I would have wept at the prospect, I would have lain on the ground in front of the bulldozer to preserve that colony of pine trees. Now, like the woodchuck who has a burrow in that field, I am only concerned with escape.

I get up and go back to Keith's smooth white door which is for a moment transformed into his face, set against me. I slap the panel with my hand, and my palm stings; the sound is minimal. "Look, I'm not going to try to make you do anything you don't want"—a lie, to gain access: he will surely smell that out. "Let's talk about this, at least, Keith. We've always been able to talk." Weakening in the face of his silence, I add, "Don't you remember, we painted your room together. We went to Hyde Park to get that bookshelf. I know how you feel."

He is silent, and I imagine him grimacing, drawing back his lips from his teeth, enraged by the quaver in my voice.

I go back to the blanket chest and sit down. There is nothing else for me to do. I remember Keith as a small boy, the sun of my life, bringing up cups of tea when I was sick in bed, running up the stairs, after school, with his hands full of crumpled drawings. Sentimentality has no thrust, in the current situation.

I return to the door, no longer a supplicant. I have run through all the changes, in five minutes; Keith has always been able to provoke me. "I'm going to get your father," I say calmly to the closed door.

There is no response, although I sense a stirring, a rustle of curiosity on the other side of the door. He will open, for a confrontation. I race down the stairs and into the kitchen, where David is waiting for his toast to pop up. His Pooh-Bear domesticity, at this moment, amazes me; he has spent the whole morning eating and drinking. I stop on my first word—"Come"—having started on the note he hates most, that of hysterical demand. I begin again, more tactfully, "Would you please come and help me? We have to do something about Keith."

He looks at the toaster. "I'm just waiting for these slices to pop up. Would you like one?"

Once, our life together was made bearable by these gestures, these small courtesies: the delicate porcelain teacups with the bluets on them, the well-chosen presents on my birthday and our anniversaries, the cab waiting at the door to bear us to city entertainments. I no longer accept these substitutes because they take the edge off my appetite for the real thing. "There is no time for toast now," I announce. "I need your help with Keith."

"What's happened?" he asks mildly, his eyes on his reflection in the toaster.

"He has barricaded himself in his room and he won't come out or let me in."

The toast pops up; David takes it gingerly and lays it on the waiting plate. Then he goes to the refrigerator to withdraw the butter. Looking in the drawer for a knife, he remarks, "Keith and I talked about all this, last night. He wants to take his things with him to my place and I told him he could."

"You can't do that, David. We agreed to this auction."

"It's your auction," he says, carefully spreading butter in order not to tear the toast. "I told you before, I feel no obligation to help you make it a success. A teenaged boy . . ." He begins, but I am no longer listening; my eyes are fixed on his short square hand, manipulating the knife.

"Everything you do now, even buttering that toast, is to get back at me," I say.

"I've noticed you've begun to interpret everything that way."

"Why did we never argue? Why did we never fight? Why didn't you tell me to stop seeing Edwin before it was too late?"

"I wanted you to be happy, and you seemed very happy, if a little hectic."

"You profited from it."

"Not finally," he says, with dignity.

"You accepted it, you wouldn't fight it, you justified my falling in love with another man. It took the pressure off you, to perform, to please me, to make some attempt at understanding. Now you've decided to punish me for it, anyhow, now you've decided to take Keith away."

"We both agreed to that."

"I had no choice, after Keith began to make my life unbearable, after you told him about Edwin."

"I don't believe there's a connection. Besides, he already knew."

"Knowing and having to confront it are two different things. Edwin is his friend's father. He can never forgive me—he'll need never to forgive me—for spoiling that friendship."

"I don't see that there's anything I can do about that."

"Back me up, give me your support. Tell him he has to go along with the plan. Tell him he has to let Tom take the furniture out of his room."

David takes a bite of toast, swallows and glances at me. "I'm not going to do that, Ann. I don't think it's fair to Keith."

I sit down suddenly at the kitchen table.

"I'll have a truck here sometime next week, to take my things, and his."

"David, what are you up to? What are you trying to do?"

"I'm thinking of the children." He wipes his fingers carefully on a bit of paper towel. At the same moment, we both glance at the yellow pad, which is lying on the counter next to the sink.

"What are you writing on that pad?" I ask. The first page is thick with his handwriting.

He glances at it, considers, thinking of timing, weighing his chances of making an impression. "I haven't seen you much, the past six months. I'm curious about some things and so I'm writing them down—observations, thoughts."

"Observations about what?"

He rinses his coffee cup and places it on the top rack of the dishwasher. "I'm trying to be fair about this, Ann—believe me. You've changed so much, since we separated. The children do need stability."

"No. It won't work, David."

He looks at me with his small smile. "I'm not so sure about that. The law has changed, you know."

"You are not going to be able to take the other two children."

"Only if it seems to be the best thing for them. Of course you could see them whenever you want."

"Not Molly and Jeff."

"We have to think about their welfare, Ann, not just about what we want. It would be a tremendous amount of work for me, taking them on fulltime. Of course I'd hire a housekeeper, a nice warm competent woman."

"Warmer and more competent than I am."

"I didn't mean that. You've done a fine job with them, especially when they were younger. But when I see the amount of friction, with Keith . . . I mean, it's just a matter of time before the other two get to your wrong side."

"My wrong side is the side I teach them from. Of course they complain. You give them everything, scduce them with presents and money and approval they haven't earned. Of course they complain about me, I set their limits."

"That's not what bothers me. You're a little erratic, Ann, you must know that. One minute screaming at them and the next smothering them with kisses. It had worried me for a long time, but it's much more pronounced lately, with the turmoil you've been going through."

"Is that the kind of thing you've been writing on your yellow pad?"

Before he answers, I reach for it—the counter is just beyond the ends of my fingers—but David is quick on his feet. He snatches the yellow pad and clasps it under his arm. "Just watch yourself," he snaps.

"You're a spy. That's what you've always been."

"Think what you want to think. I have some thoughts, too. You kept me away from the children, all those years."

"You kept yourself away. You were always busy. Even when you were around, you were preoccupied. Remember when Jeff was a baby? I was going mad, up at night with him for six months. I pleaded with you to take some time off, to help me out. You told me to hire a nurse. I didn't want a nurse. I didn't want another woman handling my baby. I wanted you to help me."

"That was in the middle of the Con Ed suit. I couldn't get away."

"Yes, I know, I know. There were always reasons, good reasons. Now suddenly you have plenty of time for them, you even have plenty of money. You never even paid their school bills, before."

"I've always contributed my fair share."

"I don't believe it. I don't understand your arrangements. The lawyers will have to straighten it all out. All I know is that you never supported us, never had money, never even told me how much you earned."

"I can't believe we're arguing about money."

"Yes, we've fallen that low. I wish to God we'd fallen that low a long time ago. It was my fault: I never would complain, to you, I felt as though I owed you my approval. I never told you how I hated you to pump away on top of me, never touching me except with your penis. I never told you how dry and hopeless it felt, neither of us coming. I never told you how I hated to spend the evening paying bills, while you watched television. I felt as though I owed you a living, an atmosphere, a whole life made by hand."

"I did take you out of a pretty desperate situation."

"You're right, I had to get away from home. And you seemed so warm, so civilized. That's what I've paid for—your civilization. The fact that you would never maul me, never make demands. I could live in my vaccuum, in my private dream, with you."

"It worked, for a while."

"Yes. But I began to know what I wanted. You still haven't begun to find out."

"I have some idea."

"I want to spend the rest of my life alone."

"I wish you'd go to one of those clinics."

"Where they fix you up with a 'partner'?"

"You can't blame me for all your misfunctions," he says wryly.

"You're right: I came to you with them." Before I can go on, he reminds me.

"We were talking about the children."

"Yes." I come back to it from a long way off. "I want you to go upstairs and talk to Keith."

"All right. I'll tell him we've settled it."

"Settled it!" I am, in a breath, beyond myself. I begin to beat my fists against his arm. "You settled it! We didn't! You sabotaged me!"

He puts my hands off, staring at me, appalled. Then he holds my two wrists together. "Ann, you are being violent. You are behaving in a violent way."

I drop my hand out of his grip.

"I thought we had settled this question about Keith, like two adults," he goes on.

"We never even discussed it. You sidetracked me. You've blown up my whole plan."

"It was never my plan," he says. Now I can see the gleam of satisfaction in his eyes.

"There's something for you to write on your yellow pad. '"Attacked by wife.'" I rub my wrists.

"I'll get Keith," he says, and leaves the kitchen.

I go to the telephone and dial my lawyer's number, in the city. His syrup-voiced secretary answers: No, Mr. Rodman is not in. No, he cannot be reached at the moment: he is in court. She will pass the message on when he returns, at some indefinite later hour. "It's urgent. Tell him to call me in the country. Something is happening here." Used to female hysteria over the telephone, she calms me expertly. Mr. Rodman will deal with everything, as soon as he returns.

I remember his sleek chrome-and-glass office, his sleek smile: a handsome man, a fighter, who only betrays his cupidity when he glances at the clock on the building outside his window. He does not have a clock on his desk. He makes it appear that we are friends—he even offers me a free cup of coffee—but while I talk, he swivels in his chair and glances out the window at the clock. There is another woman, sitting among the potted plants in the glass-and-chrome waiting room.

I am used to such timing. Edwin used to lay his watch on the table beside the bed, where he could see it while we made love.

Keith comes into the kitchen in front of his father, propelled along by his will.

"I'm sorry if I made you mad," he says.

I speak to David. "How do you expect the other children to behave, now?"

"They don't need to know, do they?"

"They're not fools. This has been hard for them, too, but they agreed; they had to. They didn't have an alternative."

"Daddy has a big apartment," Keith says mildly.

"Yes. He can afford one. He's been saving money for fifteen years."

David said, "This is simply not appropriate, Ann."

"Do you know why I had to leave you, finally? It was because you couldn't feel. No, that's not true. You can feel. But you never would let me in."

"That's a neat reason. Keith, would you like some ginger ale?"

"I learned what I wanted, finally," I say. "Maybe too late."

"The children have paid quite a price for that." He opens the bottle for Keith and pours a cup.

"More to write on the yellow pad," I say.

Keith says, carefully, "Well, it's true, you weren't around much, all last year. You were never home when I came home from school."

"You're thirteen years old. You don't need me at the door, with cookies."

"It was hard on Molly and Jeff, too," Keith says.

"Everything is hard on everybody. That's something your father won't understand. You blame everyone else for consequences, but they're not avoidable. From the moment you draw your first breath, you're caught in a maze of consequences. There is no safe place."

"That's a dangerous philosophy, with small children," David says, turning towards the living room. Keith turns, too, as though attached by an invisible tow-line.

"It is not a philosophy. It's reality, which is different."

"I intend to protect my children from it," David says. They both go into the living room and sit down side by side on the sofa.

Panic is a small mouthful; I swallow it down. To protect myself, I remember the delights that caused all this to begin: walking in the woods with Edwin, for example. He held me in his arms under the big sycamore at the edge of the pond and asked me to be patient. It was the only grain of hope he ever gave me, the only link to a future. We paid a very high price for that. Hope, after all, is beyond value.

Tom comes in the door, his hands hanging, looking around for something more to take out.

"There's the sofa," I say.

"I'll have to get Fred, for that. What about upstairs?"

"Everything except what's in the room at the end of the hall."

"We have everything else."

"All right, then take the sofa."

He looks at David and Keith. "I was leaving that to the last, so you people would have some place to sit."

"This is the last," I say, and he smiles, too, a little embarrassed, not sure where the joke lies, not sure—anymore than I am—whether or not it is a joke, at all.

# 6.

Flora began to call the children. "Saul! Keith! Peter! Chrissy —all of you! Come and open the presents!" She had assembled them in a pile beside the unlit fire. From the swings, from their clubhouse behind the woodshed, from the porch, the children came, the younger ones running, the older boys strolling as though they hardly cared at all. The three girls came, looking as though they were carrying secrets; they had been plotting something by the vegetable garden. Looking at the children, I imagined the way each one of them had begun, on a night after a party, in the middle of a hot afternoon. It seemed unlikely that any of us could remember exactly when, or why, our children had been conceived. Chance, good temper, a fatal spurt of optimism had together or separately produced this little band, tumbling or running or pacing steadily down the hill to the fire.

As they came closer, I noticed how pale and ragged they looked, in their bleached hand-me-down clothes—a Pied Piper's rabble. There were no real friendships between them, other than that between Saul and Jeff. They hung together only as a group, reflecting the grownups' precarious unity. When we were not getting along, the children fell apart and sulked in corners. When we were excited, feeding off a new alliance, a new argument, a new affair, the children fought and laughed indiscriminately. "The grownups are the children," I told Edwin once, pontificating to stop my distress at the sight of their random willingness to be drawn in. That was after Chrissy had telephoned the doctor in town because Sheila was choking on a chicken bone; all the adults were off walking in the woods. The doctor advised bread, and the crisis had passed by the time we returned. "Thank God we get to be the children," Edwin had said, not to be shamed.

Saul, a knobbly nine-year-old, Edwin's youngest, squatted down by the pile of presents and ripped into the first one. "Read the card," Flora reminded him crisply; she hated any display of greed. Saul stopped ripping and began to poke around for the card. Jeff had drawn it, painstakingly, complaining of the bumps in the road, when we were driving up from the city. Saul found the card and showed it around, to polite exclamations: a huge mouth, without teeth, shouting, "Happy birthday!" I was glad there were no teeth. As Saul handed me the card, I caught his eye, by accident, and he looked hastily away; the children were as unused to direct looks as cats. Saul had his father's eyes, pale grey, wary and bright, the eyes of an animal drawn against its instincts into company. Those eyes brought me instantly to my stored images of Edwin, images which prodded me out of bed in the morning, to work, to flourish, to continue to earn his interest, images which propelled me on my rounds, into the subway, onto buses, picking up the children, and which stood finally like shining angels between me and my own perception of my life.

Monday—five days before—Edwin had rushed in my front door, late, as always, with only half an hour to spare for me, between appointments. He stripped off his watch and laid it where he could see it, on the table beside my bed, then stood with his arms stretched out so that I could unbutton his blue-and-white striped shirt. He submitted to my touch with ill-grace, fearful that I would leave a trace or smell, which would be detected by Flora. In spite of that, I seized him, with his clothes on. His armor was so thick and smooth that I could not believe a trace of mine would cling. Unbuttoning his shirt, I put my cold hands on his chest, so warm and smooth, so vulnerable to me. Then I unbuckled his worn leather belt, unzipped his fly, and in panic—stricken by greed—reached for his cock, already stiffening, rising to meet my fingers. Standing, I held his cock between my thighs, cradling it, feeling it jerk and then lift smoothly against the closed lips of my cunt, I got down on my knees and took him in my mouth; he was smooth, tough, pulsing, very sweet. For the first time in my life, I was taking a man as I wanted to be taken, with zest, with the full range of my desire. Edwin allowed me. I believed it was only a matter of time before he would take me in the same way, slowly, tonguing me first, helping me to come.

Saul was ravaging his presents, throwing paper and ribbons in the air. Flora shouted, "Stop that at once!" She did not want Saul to let us see that he did not really care about the presents; once ripped open, he threw them aside. Flora insisted that he look at each one again and thank each child. She knew the effort those meaningless toys represented— afternoons in stores while our own children fretted, unwilling to choose anything for a potential rival. The cards meant something because they were homemade. Flora gathered them up, to keep. We had bullied our children to produce a rudimentary drawing or collage, to conform to Flora's expectations. She made everything she gave away herself, and my shelves were blessed by her blueberry jam and cucumber pickle, too precious to be eaten.

Edwin went around collecting the wrapping paper and stuffing it under the logs. Crouching, he struck a match. The flame travelled rapidly up though the paper and sticks; the logs began to pop; soon the fire was burning vigorously and a thin column of smoke rose through the faded air. Edwin began to sharpen sticks with his pocketknife, to use for hot dogs.

Flora and Helena settled themselves near the food and began to deal out paper plates. Flora's voice, scolding, rose over the crackling fire. "You boys are pigs—don't snatch. Peter, one potato chip at a time. Jeff, you know better than to put your whole hand in the pickle jar. No marshmallow now for you, Chrissy, those are for later. Don't stuff your mouth! Wait for the rolls! Really," she looked at me, rolling her eyes, "they are disgusting." I smiled back at her. She always scolded more on weekends when Edwin and I had fucked during the previous week.

Trying to stay away from Edwin, I sat down by my husband. He speared a hot dog on a stick, then poked it into the fire. He did not need to tell me that he was taking care of me even before he took care of himself. I snatched the stick out of his hand and he glanced at me curiously. If I rejected his care, his courtesy, he had nothing else to offer. I poked the stick deep into the fire, then pulled it back—too late: the hot dog blazed up, sputtering.

"Give me another," I told Edwin. He got up and went to get one from Flora, pleased to be allowed, after all, to serve. For a while, we were all as absorbed as the children in getting our hotdogs cooked and eaten. Charles went around with a jug of wine, refilling our paper cups; the children, as a special treat, were being given what Flora called, "that Nasty Punch—full of chemicals." The grownups, at last, would be half-drunk and nearly gay by the middle of the afternoon.

Peter took my cup without asking permission and gulped a mouthful of wine. That made Flora fierce. She shrieked at Edwin to stop him. Edwin, sitting on the other side of the fire, diddling his hotdog over the coals, told Peter without force to behave. "How can I teach them anything when you—" Flora began, then chopped off the rest. She and I had seen as though with the same eyes Helena get up and move over to sit by Edwin.

The air seemed to stiffen and crack. Charles began at once to lecture. At first I did not understand what he was talking about, although I picked out each word.

Charles' conversations were monologues, leading to fore-ordained conclusions—in this case, that we should all petition the village fathers to ban the use of minibikes in the woods. We were walkers except for Charles, who kept a horse and fancied himself in riding boots; one of the minibikes, careening through the woods, had frightened his horse and caused him a nasty fall. He delineated its owner, an overgrown high school student who collected mechanical junk in his front yard and lived in the euphoria of loud noises. I allowed my-self to look at Edwin. He had edged closer to Helena and they were talking together.

For five minutes, I did not allow myself to look back. I was unprepared for this: jealousy notched me. It was daytime, after all. At evening parties, I had made myself accustomed, almost numb, to Edwin's flirting; like Flora, I tried to look away from the bewitched smiles which he shed on other women, indiscriminately, or according to a rule or impulse which neither Flora nor I had been able to divine. Usually, in the daytime, he was too busy to make the effort. Pain gripped my hands, seizing them and knotting them up. I reminded myself that Edwin and Helena were old comrades, old friends—as Edwin and I had been. Edwin had helped Helena through Chrissy's bedwetting crisis, as he had helped me to understand Jeff's stammering. In the sudden silence, Charles was still lecturing. "I mean, why should we all be sacrificed . . . Peace of mind," he added, abruptly, as though he saw it shining a long way off. David handed me another hotdog, perfectly roasted.

After a while, I allowed myself to look again. Edwin was leaning towards Helena, his face a few inches from her face. They had stopped talking. Helena closed her eyes. She tilted her face slightly, bringing her mouth in line with Edwin's lips. His face, as though magnetized, tilted, too. His eyes were closed. In the firelight, he looked blank and tense, a sleep-walker edging a precipice.

Flora said, "I'm going to get the coffee." She lunged up and started for the house.

Charles began to instruct David in the usefulness of the local zoning laws.

I crept to my husband and leaned against his knee, curled like a snail. I did not look at Edwin. After a long time, I heard Flora coming back, swinging a clanking pail of coffee mugs. "Coffee?" she asked brusquely, squatting in front of me to fill a mug. She held the handle of the big tin coffee pot firmly in a teatowel. "Disgusting," she murmured as she handed me the mug, with a shrug and a grimace towards her husband.

I looked again, under her custody. Their faces seemed to be two halves of the same sphere, moving in unison. Helena's lips were open. They did not quite touch Edwin's mouth.

"Otherwise people who enjoy horses will simply have to live somewhere else," Charles concluded gloomily. David nodded, in agreement.

"It's the buildup I hate," Flora told me.

I was sick. My stomach was crawling. I wanted to go to Edwin and interpose my body between his and Helena's. He had had me and he continued to have me, regularly—I fed him; but it was never enough.

"I'm going to take the question up with the mayor. Shipley has some sense, even if he is a plumber," Charles told David.

Flora spooned sugar into my mug. She had taken upon herself the role of comforter: I hated her for it. She made it impossible for me to believe what I wanted to believe: that what Edwin was doing was nothing. But then death was nothing. I could see the transfixed delight on his face, the look he hid from me when he came.

Flora began to pick up the paper plates, although some of the children had not finished eating. She ordered them to help, but except for Chrissy, who went on methodically chewing, the children took one look at Flora's face and abandoned their meal, running off and shouting back that they were going to play tag. I had never seen Flora's will flouted before. She was biting her lips, her face graven. "Monsters," she said, stuffing paper napkins into the basket. Charles and David began to gather up the bottles. In the midst of our activity, Edwin and Helena preserved their island of calm. We flitted around them, talking, united by our pretense that nothing was happening. Edwin's hand sat quietly on Helena's knee.

"We're going up to the house," Flora sang, to no one in particular, and we trooped after her, leaving Edwin and Helena by the fire, with Chrissy, who was still chewing.

In the kitchen, we all fell silent. The men piled the remains on the table and went off to the living room to look for cigarettes. "It doesn't mean anything, it never does," Flora told me, her forehead close to mine as we crammed paper plates into the garbage pail. "I'm going to give up using paper plates after this, look at the disgusting waste, I hate to think of the trees. . ."

I was afraid that she was going to begin to cry.

Chrissy ran in, full tilt, slammed a ginger ale bottle on the table and was nearly out the door again when I caught her arm. "Is there anything left, down there by the fire?"

Headed away, she did not turn around. "Mommy and Edwin are bringing up the rest of the stuff."

The intimacy of their cleaning up together, bringing things up to the house together, hurt me more than the aborted kiss. Pain took me again. Like a seizure, it created around it silence and the imminence of shame. I knew that I had to find a place to be alone, before I broke down in Flora's arms. I started for the stairs.

"Where are you going?" she called after me.

"Upstairs."

For a minute, I was afraid she would follow me. Then I heard water running in the sink.

At the top of the stairs, I went into Flora's and Edwin's bedroom, a chilly little room, shaped by the eaves.

74 ]

On their bed, the telephone, the newspaper and several piles of folded laundry lay mixed together. I moved some of the clothes in order to sit down. Edwin's faded blue undershorts were on the top of one pile.

I reached for them and opened them out. The elastic in the waist was limp and the cotton felt thin. I seized the material in my teeth. The cotton did not give as easily as I had expected. I drew it into my mouth, sucking and chewing. Wet, it seemed thicker yet and more resistant. I spat it out, took the pants between my hands and, with all my strength, ripped them in two from the bottom of the fly to the waistband in back.

I sat holding them for a while. My hands would not come ungripped. The sound of the tearing lingered and my mouth tasted soft and dry, like the cotton.

Standing up, I threw the rag on the floor and knocked it under the bed with the side of my foot. I began to walk towards the door. As I approached it, I saw Jeff standing beside the bureau, shrinking into its shadow. I looked away. In the kitchen, Flora was crashing pans; I went down to join her. After a while, I saw Jeff slip down the stairs and disappear outside.

# 7.

Tom and Fred are walking towards the sofa. David gets up, Keith, too, after a little. I look at the room as though for the last time. It is my favorite place in the house—the room where everything happened. The children used to play here while I cooked; in winter, this was the fireplace we lighted (it always smoked; there is a dark stain under the mantel) and when the Fields came to dinner, this is the table I opened out and filled with all its leaves. The big white pediments over the doors and windows, the pale yellow walls make a frame now for a picture which no longer exists.

Veering off from the sofa, Tom inspects the rest of the furniture, huddled in the corner. He is checking for red tags, which mean that the object is not for sale. "The only thing in here with a tag is that love seat," I tell him and smile at his relief. He did not believe me when I told him that I would not keep all the good things; he wanted to go over the house with me, to make sure. I refused. The deal almost collapsed then. I couldn't bear to go through my things in company with his thick face and the stink of his beer breath. The few things I am keeping are not valuable; I want them because they are attached to stories.

Of course everything in the house has a story of some sort—a rainy day at an auction, at the very least—but most of the stories are trivial and a few are no longer bearable. The beds, for instance: I will never sleep in any of these beds again because of the furies of hope that attacked me there. Most of the things which my family gave me have gradually shed their meaning, losing color as my life has taken it on, except for my grandmother's loveseat, its mahogany back arched like a wave. I used to sit there, uncomfortably perched on the slippery horsehair, while she unwound her stories. Under a light coating of Southern charm—slippers with rose-colored linings and rose-colored heels, brides like lighted candles—her stories were about horror and mayhem, murder and particularly, rape. My grandmother prepared me for the ways of the world, teaching me to accept lies out of a steadfast terror of the truth—"She died beautifully, beautifully; they never knew the cause"—to accept excuses rather than reasons—"They said he shot her in the throat, but when her diary was finally read . . ."—caution rather than conviction and, above all, to choose what is known. My grandmother never left her state, and she considered women who did gallivanting fools who deserved whatever calamity befell them. When a friend of hers was mugged in New York, Grandmother had no sympathy. "I told Matilda before she left here, she was making a mistake." Some of her wisdom clings to me still, and since it protected me for most of my life, I plan to keep her loveseat, which I have recovered with brown corduroy.

Tom and Fred begin to pull the sofa towards the door. Molly comes from the parlor to watch; her father and her brother pass her, in retreat. "Is he taking everything in here?" Molly asks.

"Everything except for Great-Grandmother's loveseat."

"Why do you want to keep that old thing?"

"I used to sit on it when Grandmother told her stories. I've told you some of them."

"Yes, that one about the woman drowned in a cask of wine, all her blonde hair hanging out and going on growing."

"They were terrible stories. I loved them."

"I don't see why you get to keep that sofa, just because somebody gave it to you," she whines, her glee vanishing as she reverts to her complaint. "Aunt Edna gave me my doll-house, I should get to keep it, too."

"I've told you several times, Molly, if you want to give up your bed and keep your dollhouse . . ."

David says, from the hall, "Let it go, Molly. We can always buy another dollhouse."

Molly runs to him, to seal the deal: my daughter who, unlike me, always knows when to press her advantage.

I try to rein in my irritation.

David says, from the doorway, "It's really too hard on her, you know."

"It's not too hard on her. Nothing is too hard on her. She's tough as nails." I stop, lining up my priorities. This is not a fight I have to win.

"I saw one in FAO Schwarz that even has an elevator!" Molly says.

"Hold on there, now." They begin to discuss the amount of money David is willing to pay—a large sum, which will buy his daughter's allegiance for at least a week. To my surprise, I hear him haggling: he wants her cheap. No elevator, he decrees. They finally settle on a house which Molly has seen in a neighborhood store; it does have stairs and a fireplace and a porch and a chimney, but it does not have an elevator.

"What about the old dollhouse, I thought you were so fond of it," I say.

"The windows are just plastic," she says airily and goes off with her father to the kitchen, hand in hand.

Fred and Tom begin to take the dinner table apart, stacking the leaves carefully against the wall. They push the two semicircular halves together and the table is as small as it was when we first lived in the house. Then there was no one to eat with us. There was a snowstorm, our first Christmas; the wind blew the snow under the kitchen door while we sat at the table, eating our small-family turkey. I cried after lunch because we had no family, except for the children, who were not enough, would never be enough, even if I continued to pump out a baby every two years. There was no ritual, no sustenance for me. At that point, we had no country friends. "You could have invited somebody," David reminded me, clearing away the plates; the children had hardly touched the food which I had spent two days preparing. "I don't want my mother," I said—I did not dare to want her: she was not available. Freed at last from the thankless task of raising a daughter who was neither a beauty nor a scholar but a self-defeating combination, a bright girl who only cared about love, she had moved to Palm Beach, growing younger and more handsome as I frayed, thriving as I shrivelled on the edge of a life that had no center. She sent us all big checks at Christmas. My grandmother, by then, was long dead, my uncle far gone in alcoholism, and so we were left with the children. They were all weaned, that first Christmas in the country.

Tom rolls the table swiftly to the front door, the castors squealing. He and Fred maneuver it onto its side and push it into the doorway. It is wedged, briefly, its goat legs in the air, before Fred with a grunt shoves it through. I wonder who will sit at it next and whether their dream of a family for grownups, united by food and love and honesty, will by some wild stroke of luck be transformed into reality.

# 8.

In the middle of a hot week, Flora telephoned to ask me whether or not I had seen Dan; her septic tank was overflowing and she was desperate. I had never met Flora and the smooth quality of her desperation awed me. She was as much in control of the contents of her septic tank—as I was of Jeff's diahrrea—that is, not at all. But Flora was detached. "Isn't it too much," she said. For me, Jeff really was too much; my eyes were raw with fatigue, my lips as dry and cracked as a nomad's. I hadn't slept through a night for almost two months. After I told Flora that I didn't know where Dan was, I realized with a pang that I had disappointed her. To make up for that, I invited her to bring her children over to swim. She replied at once that she couldn't stand swimming pools— "All that concrete"—but would be pleased to welcome me at the little pond which Edwin had dug with a rented bulldozer. There was clearly no argument and again I felt almost embarrassed, as though Flora was a finger pointing a finer way.

At first glance, Flora's size impressed me. Standing on the raw edge of the little pond, wearing a pastel bathing suit of the kind my mother called Dressmaker, she seemed to have been planted to the ankle in the dirt and I was not surprised when she did not step forward to speak to me. She waited, and I went to her and held out my hand, which she took in a limp grasp, graciously. Her pale, rather small blue eyes checked me over carefully, looking for a certain signal, or detail. I did not know whether or not I passed, but I knew my bikini was not correct for that patch of brown water and sun. My children lingered behind me, looking askance at Flora's three who were skirmishing in the water.

"I'm sorry I couldn't find Dan," I said.

"Never mind. I've called Edwin and he's coming up on the four o'clock train."

"Meanwhile—"

"Meanwhile—" Wrinkling her nose, she indicated the putrid stench which seemed to edge the air we shared. "Meanwhile I suppose we will simply have to put up with the smell." She led me to a picnic bench, set at an angle in the mud, as though she was leading me to a throne.

"Get out of there!" she shouted at her children, so suddenly I jumped. They jumped as well, and assembled, dripping and fidgeting, a little distance from my feet. She introduced them formally—"Saul, Frank, Seth"—and I shook their slippery hands and then introduced Molly and Keith. They were small brown creatures that summer, their hair bleached white; indistinguishable—"And the baby?" Flora asked reprovingly. Jiggling him in my arms, I gave him his name as though for the first time.

"Get back into the water," Flora ordered and her children dove in at once, followed, at a little distance, by Keith and Molly who stood in the shallows and watched while the others ostentatiously splashed and screamed.

"The noise!" Flora threw up her eyes. "Shall we go up to the house?"

"And leave them in the water? I don't generally—"

"Yours don't swim?"

"Molly doesn't, not yet, really—she's only four."

"Absolutely essential for them to learn to swim. You must take them down to the village on Monday; they give lessons at the American Legion Pond. Now, you can sit by the kitchen window and watch their every move." I followed her up the hill to the little grey house.

Inside, Flora fixed glasses of iced tea, dilating on her dislike of the instant kind, which Frank had managed to buy behind her back at the IGA. He had slipped it into her cart at the last moment and she had nearly missed it. "Nothing but chemicals," she said grimly. "I made him pay for it."

My arms were tired from holding Jeff, who was stamping up and down on my lap. "Will you hold this baby a minute?" I asked. Flora looked surprised, but she held out her hands, and I placed Jeff between them.

Jeff took one look at Flora and gave an indignant roar. She patted his back, expertly and remotely. "Gas, I expect."

"But I'm nursing—there's no air."

"Oh, you're one of those," she said good-naturedly, glancing at my shirt which was stained, under my left nipple, by a damp patch of milk.

"I've nursed all of mine," I said.

"Edwin never would make that sacrifice."

Dismayed, I explained that I had never met her husband.

"You will, presently," she said. "He'll be here a little after six, to deal with this mess. Of course he'll have to go right back to town in the morning."

"I won't be staying that long, it's only three, now," I protested.

"Why don't we all have supper goether? We can fix spaghetti," she said. "It would give the children a chance to make friends." Flattered, I still hesitated, thinking of my own dinner and the early evening alone; dismal, peaceful and fast slipping away. "After all, we're all in this together," she went on. "There's absolutely not one person to see up here—which is why we chose this place! To be private." She seemed to shine the word and hold it at arm's length to admire it. "But of course, the children must have friends."

In the end, I stayed to supper. The children had already begun to form alliances by the time they came up from the pool; Molly, the only girl, had been accepted as a mascot and a crybaby because Keith saved her when the others were holding her under the water. Frank, a sad, shabby nine-year-old with a fringe of wet hair in his eyes, had the distinction of his unhappiness; he was tormented by his brothers and yet respected because he was the one most apt to get into trouble and once in trouble, to cry. As for Keith, he was still, I noticed, on his guard; he stood in the angle of the kitchen walls and watched the other children darting like swallows with their plates of spaghetti. My eldest had always been the leader at home and I saw that he now felt too evenly matched, for prestige. I was delighted by the easy way Flora's three were interweaving with mine; there was material here for several summers. The weight of my loneliness began to lift.

They all managed to crowd onto kitchen chairs, around the table, dripping water as they ate. "Not on my clean floor, you beasts," Flora objected, but they refused to dry outside, shouting together as though they had practiced it. Flora rapidly spread newspaper under their feet. My baby was howling again, after a brief, jerking nap, and I asked Flora if I could nurse him in the kitchen. She glanced at me with a startling wince of distaste. "Edwin feels very strongly that the children shouldn't be exposed to that sort of thing."

I stood up. "Then I'll go upstairs."

She began to explain rapidly, "It's not that I disapprove, you understand. Edwin simply feels that sort of thing is too stimulating for the boys. He feels it's one of the most difficult things about the way we live; the children are constantly stirred up and overexcited. They hardly have a chance at latency . . . Make yourself comfortable on our bed, I'll take care of supper."

Climbing the narow stairs, my irritation died. After all, I thought, Flora was right to insist on her opinions, or her husband's. So few people had convictions, it seemed to me, either their own or shared. Yet there had been an oddly artificial tinge to Flora's voice, as though she was speaking from the book. I wondered if she often quoted Edwin. I had heard, casually, that he was a well-regarded child analyst and so of course it was perfectly appropriate that he should guide his children and instruct his wife. Yet the hint of shellac bothered me. I wondered if Flora had only been trying to explain her spasm of distaste.

I went into a low dim room, under the eaves, still stuffed with heat from the long day. I oared the air away with one arm, making my way to the unmade double bed. The pillows were heaped up on one edge, and a pile of laundry lay across the foot. As I sat down and arranged the pillows, with one hand, behind my head, I suddenly realized that I had no business there. The room reeked of intimacy. It was as though each shabby and ordinary object—the telephone, the newspaper, a broken-spined paperback—was covered with luminous fingerprints. At once I remembered the particular smell of my parents' pillows; on the sly, I used to bury my nose in them, learning to distinguish my mother's dry sour stink from my father's leathery reek. Sitting bolt upright, I resisted the impulse to turn and sink my face into these pillows. They are strangers!, I thought to myself. Still sitting up, I unbuttoned my shirt and nursed the baby distractedly, trying to sort out the afternoon, hardly aware, for the first time, of the delicious prickling of my milk.

As I was finishing, I heard a car turn into the gate. I leaned over to look out of the little low window. A car door slammed.

Almost at the same moment, the screen door clapped and I saw Flora flash out. She ran towards the car. Once, she jumped and skipped like a rabbit. I stared. I saw her hold out her arms and then a man in a dark suit disappeared briefly behind her face. As he emerged, I saw his smile, pale and rather set.

They came towards the house hand-in-hand, Flora talking rapidly.

I buttoned my shirt, snatched up the baby and hurried down the stairs, shouting for my children.

In the kitchen, Keith was doling out big scoops of ice cream: the younger children stood around him in a circle, holding out their bowls. "We can't go home yet!" Molly wailed as soon as she saw me. As I argued, Flora came in the door, leading Edwin by the wrist. With a graceful gesture, she released him and tapped him gently in my direction. I was struck by his dazed stare; he hardly seemed to notice me as Flora spoke my name. I held out my hand. He took it briefly and looked at me briefly and coolly. The skin of his palm, under my fingertips, felt worn and finegrained.

"I must go," I said.

"Stay, and have supper with us. We'll get these monsters to bed and have some quiet time, later," Flora sang.

Edwin said nothing.

"But you must want to talk—"

"Plenty of time for that," Edwin said suddenly, with a grin that came and went rapidly, leaving his face unchanged.

I stayed, in spite of myself. The ambiguity of the welcome seemed to enhance it; I felt that I was wanted and not wanted about equally. The atmosphere which had dismayed me in the bedroom seemed to be spreading solidly through the house. Edwin made us all whiskeys without asking our preference; I noticed his fine small hands as he broke the ice out of the tray. He took off his jacket—it had a light blue stripe— and hung it carefully on one of the cabinet knobs. That seemed to be a signal; he stretched, and threw back his head to yawn. I noticed his shoulderblades as he reached over his head; the tails of his shirt pulled out and I saw the edge of his blue shorts, crumpled against the pale skin of his back. He took a drink, and smiled at me. "So you're one of Dan's, too? I hope he's been better with you, less of a disappointment. I expect he would try harder with a lady. I must reach him now about this mess, or should I say this stink?" He strode, with relish, to the telephone. As he was dialing, Seth came and hung around his waist; Edwin put down the receiver and crouched to receive the little boy's embrace. He nuzzled and squeezed Seth and then, suddenly, glanced at me.

"Have some spaghetti," Flora said, and heaped my plate. "How are you finding your first summer in the country?"

"It's very lonely," I said and realized that was the simple truth which I had been hiding for six weeks under my lists and my chores, my gardening and my sewing and my homemade blackcap jelly.

"You must come over here whenever you want; the children will become friends, they'll amuse each other; it will make life much easier for all of us. We'll plan the summer together," she said with such warmth that I was stunned.

Edwin put Seth away gently and dialed again. He began a conversation with Dan which was very long and very funny; I gathered that from the way Edwin shifted his weight and smiled. He could have been listening to an old boyhood friend. I understood now why the Fields' house had been the first of the four houses to be finished.

Flora settled down across the table from me with her plate of spaghetti. Turning, she flapped the last children out of the kitchen. Then she bent her attention on me. "Have you met the Jacobis yet?"

"They have the new house on Miller Road, don't they?"

"Yes. It's just like ours—except it's a horrible shade of brown. The children are very rude about it. Gordon is all right—Edwin knows him professionally. But I don't believe I'm going to be able to tolerate Wiggy. It is a shame when people like that decide to move to the country. They really don't like it, they don't know what to do, and they impose themselves on their friends. Besides, any grown woman who allows herself to be called Wiggy—"

"They have a green Mercedes," Frank said, passing through with a flashlight.

"Here in the country!" Flora remarked. "Too much money—it is hard to bear. Wiggy has a different creation on every time I see her; even in the IGA, her nails are painted, and her toenails, too. I always thought that was the height. They will drop in without telephoning ahead."

"I hate that fat Arnold," Frank said, still hovering. "He's always breaking my models and then he says he'll pay me for them."

"Hush. Go out of here. Your father is on the telephone." As Frank left, Flora said, "The boys are horrible about them. Yet it is really quite disgusting. They give Arnold and Betsy five dollars a week each for pocket money and they have absolutely no responsibilities."

"It sounds as though you'd be better off without them."

"Yes, but they will drop in. Edwin encourages them. He feels sorry for Wiggy. Apparently she's going through some kind of crisis."

"Premenopausal," Edwin said, hanging up the telephone. "A good deal pre—. Also she has nice legs. Ben says he'll be here with the pump truck in half an hour."

We both exclaimed. "How did you do it?" Flora asked.

Edwin smiled, and I saw his eye teeth, set like seeds in his wide, thin-lipped mouth. "You know my charm!"

"I thought it only worked on women."

"I have my way with men, too. Always have."

"Now don't be disgusting." With a rapid motion, Flora snatched all the plates off the table. "How am I going to teach the boys not to boast, if you go on that way?"

"I must get them to come down with me."

"Don't you want to eat, first?"

"No, I don't—hardly!" He was pulling on a pair of black rubber boots, tucking up the legs of his trousers. Then he was gone; I heard him calling the children outside. I glanced at Flora. She had stopped what she was doing and was standing empty-handed at the sink, frowning at the paper towel roller. It was as though the light, which had been failing, had suddenly gone completely out of the room.

Flora snapped on the light switch. "These long country evenings when it's always getting dark!" The bare bulb, dangling from the ceiling, flooded us with hard light, and the darkness outside thickened. I heard the children yodeling away down the hill.

"He's such a child," Flora said. "Yet sometimes I'm jealous of the children."

We began the washing up. Flora moved slowly as though suddenly exhausted. She would not let me load the dishwasher, explaining succinctly that she had her own system.

She began to talk after a while. "Sometimes I'm positively jealous of the children. Edwin spends so much time with them—his patients, who are children, and our children. He cares enormously about them. I used to feel . . . squeezed out." She gave her shoulders a shake. "That was in the beginning, when they were small. I used to watch him holding them in his arms . . . Yes, it was jealousy," she said firmly. "And then how can I teach them anything, when he's so impossible?"

"What do you mean?"

"Oh—he likes the naughtiness in them."

"He encourages them?"

"He certainly does." She said it with pride. "I mean, of course we agree, basically," she added. "But he lets them be little monkeys, sometimes, and of course they love it. I'm the one who has to see to the discipline. He'd let them grow up anyhow."

A little later, we heard splashes from the direction of the pond. Flora looked at me. "You see? That's the kind of thing I mean. They should be getting ready to go to bed."

After a while, I went out to collect my children. The thick soft country closed around me as I moved slowly, feeling my way down the hill towards the pond. The children were all in the shallows; I saw their white buttucks and thighs as they jumped and cavorted in the headlights from the car, which Edwin had driven to the edge of the pond. Edwin was standing in the water with Molly clinging to his back, her arms around his neck, her long legs wrapped around his waist. He was cupping her little round buttocks in his hands. I called to my children, panic-stricken, from the darkness, and Edwin sank quickly into the water, releasing Molly, who floated away from him like a petal. The two boys came scuttling, alarmed by my voice, but it was a long time before I could draw Molly out. Finally I went to stand and scold at the edge of the pond. Edwin was swimming at the deep end, by that time, enthralled with his boys.

I realized I would never be able to find the children's clothes and shoes, thrown down on the grass in the dark. They huddled against me, shivering, subdued. Suddenly it seemed very late, later than we had ever been out before. "It's miles past your bedtimes and you're going to catch colds," I scolded, herding them towards the car. It seemed minor, somehow, to be worrying about pants and shoes when the night was so soft and the other children were shouting with excitement and glee. My own life, and my children's, looked shrunken by comparison; it would never have occurred either to me or to David to take them swimming naked in the dark.

As we went to the car, Flora came hurrying behind us with an armload of towels. "Here, wrap them up in these—don't worry about their clothes! Come by in the morning and pick them up."

I got them into the backseat, covered them with the towels, and started the car. As I turned out of the gates, I nearly collided with the pump truck, lumbering along. As the driver shouted at me, "Watch where you're going, can't you?" I thought I heard in his voice my own excitement. The dead days were done.

# 9.

December, almost a year ago: Mary Cassaday had invited us to a dinner party—I had been living off expectation for two weeks. During that time, Molly came down with impetigo, Jeff was at home for a week with the flu and my husband cancelled a business trip I'd been counting on him to take. Mary Cassaday's invitation, a pale-blue note with her hand-writing streaming across it, consoled me for everything—dear Mary, the true mother of invention, who would spend two days cooking in order to provide me with an excuse to see Edwin. In the city, he had been very busy; he did not return my calls. I knew better than to complain. So Mary's pale-blue note was as large a factor in my life as the presence of the children—perhaps larger. I knew Edwin and Flora were going because Flora had asked me to buy her a new dress to wear to the party.

Flora was teaching and had no time for inessentials. She had always hated shopping anyway. Although she was a size larger and several inches taller than I—occasionally in my dreams she loomed like a mountain—I was able to choose clothes for her unerringly. They were never quite right but they seemed to point the way towards a good change. So on the day of the party, I took her a substantial brown-and-white box, lined with tissue paper and tied with a white ribbon.

She looked at the box disapprovingly when I laid it on her kitchen table. "I hate to think how much that must have cost."

The children had gone fishing with their father and the house was quiet.

"Wait till you see the dress, it's worth every penny—you told me you wanted something well-made." I took off the box top, folded back the tissue paper and revealed the surprise: a handsome clinging black woolen dress with a jacket to conceal the décolletage. Flora looked at the dress as though it might strike her. "Try it on," I urged. Her unwillingness was part of her charm, like her thick brown hair. She was neither a liar nor a hypocrite, would not spare her own feelings or anyone else's, and her honesty, once accepted, proved decorative. She began slowly to unbutton her denim shirt.

Her big breasts, pink-nippled and drooping, flashed as she pulled off her shirt. I looked away. Flora's fleshiness was an aspect of our situation which I was trying to ignore. She was, too clearly, my opposite. Where I was flat or even concave, she was full and round; her belly would have filled my indentation, her popped naval, relic of three pregnancies, would have stoppered my curved niche. Together, we might have made a whole. Carefully, she unbuttoned her blue jeans and slid down the zipper. To please Edwin, she did not wear underpants. Her dark curling pubic hair caught in the zipper. She untangled it methodically. As she leaned over to push down her jeans, her buttocks gleamed in the ordinary air. My God, I thought, she's beautiful: he rides her.

I did not help her lift the evening dress out of the box.

She dropped the dress over her head and turned for me to zip up the back. Edwin must always zip her zippers, for her to turn so trustingly for help. Feeling at the neckline, she said discontentedly, "It's much too low-cut. Edwin won't like it."

"I know. That's why there's a jacket." I held up the little garment for her to slip in her arms. She pinched the front closed tightly with one hand, then turned to survey herself in the glass door. It was difficult to see anything except dark shifting planes. "Don't you have a mirror?"

"Just Edwin's shaving mirror, in the bathroom, and that won't do much good."

Watching her turn uneasily, fingering the dress, I wondered whether Edwin's prudishness grew out of her unease, or whether he had imposed on her the image she now held as though with the tips of her fingers: a large woman, very competent, and by her virtues entirely unsuited to a black evening dress.

"It's tight over the hips," she complained.

"No, it isn't. It fits perfectly."

"Edwin doesn't like me to wear anything tight."

"I know that, Silly."

"I'll try it on again later," she said, turning her back for me to unzip her. "Maybe I'll like it better. You wouldn't mind frightfully returning it, would you?"

I slid down the zipper and looked at her broad white back. That was a safe zone. "Of course I'll take it back. That's our deal." Suddenly I was annoyed and I wondered why I was always dressing Flora. Of course she paid me.

"How much did it cost?" she asked suspiciously, turning away to put on her clothes.

"One hundred and fifteen." Without thinking, I had cut thirty-five dollars off the price.

"That's terrible!"

"Not really," I began to show her the seams. "You'll be able to wear it for years."

"I have the money, of course, but I do resent spending it on clothes."

"I know, but this is an investment." I heard the servile saleswoman's whine in my voice. "Look, Flora, if you don't like it . . ."

"Oh, I like it, it's very smart. It's just so different from what I ordinarily wear."

"It's time for you to get rid of that old corduroy skirt," I said, brusque as a mother.

"Edwin likes it."

"I don't care whether he likes it or not. It's not flattering."

She dropped the black dress back into the box. "I dread to think what you'll be wearing."

"Only my old white dress."

"Your old white dress! They won't be able to take their eyes off you."

"Who?" I asked, entering into the game.

"Oh, you know." Our eyes met briefly, conspiratorially; we were little girls sharing a dolls' tea party. "Have a cup of coffee," Flora said. "You know very well who I mean." She was ready to expand the game.

I laughed, to stop her, and sat down at the kitchen table while she fetched the cups. She knew better than to follow that line of inquiry. Instead, she began to complain about Saul, who was doing badly in school. A line of vexation settled between her eyes. Generally her children were a credit to her, quiet, well-mannered, tuned to a meager reality (except when they were with Edwin, and Flora took no responsibility for that). Saul had recently sloughed off part of his training, becoming, for the time being, a roughneck. Someone had reported seeing him sneaking on the back door of the Broadway bus. "Edwin won't take it seriously," Flora complained. "You know how he is."

"He doesn't like to scold."

"Except when it's Frank. He's after him all the time, he won't leave him alone. Frank cries easily."

I thought of Frank's long pale face. At eleven, he was a forlorn version of his father, hungry, lacking Edwin's charm. Frank caught his first cold in September and kept it until spring, and Edwin could make him cry at any hour of the night or day simply by reminding him of the grades he made in French. The other children drifted off one by one when Edwin began to point out their faults—he was always fair about it, and even asked them afterwards what they had felt when he lectured; still they drifted off to listen to the stereo through headphones or do their homework until only Frank was left, a thin figure of misery, staring at his father through streaming tears. He was a courageous child, the only one of the three who always looked Edwin in the face.

"Sometimes Edwin frightens me," Flora confided. "Last night, he hit Frank and knocked him down."

I gasped. Edwin's violence had never flowered in front of me although I had felt it, root and stem, in all his lovemaking. "What did you do?"

"Nothing. What could I do? Trying to stop Edwin only makes him worse. I've learned that, at least, in fifteen years."

"Poor Frank," I muttered, stunned by her complicity.

"He has to learn to be tough." She stood up, dashing the rest of her coffee into the sink. "He'll never get by, snivelling and crying."

"He's only eleven."

"That has nothing to do with it. He simply won't make any effort. He's not doing at all well in school this semester."

I stood up suddenly.

She glanced at me. "Don't leave. I need you to help me with the cakes. You can beat the eggs."

"I have to go home and fix lunch."

"Let David fix lunch, for once."

"I have to go."

She looked back at her recipe. "I wish you wouldn't. Edwin will be coming soon, with the boys, he'll be so disappointed if you aren't here."

"Don't you ever want to do what he does, Flora?"

She considered it from afar. "Well, of course sometimes I'm curious. Edwin's the only man I've ever had. I'd like to see what it's like, with somebody else, before I'm too old. But Edwin feels I'd probably get involved, emotionally, if I tried it."

"So he doesn't permit it."

"It's not like that, it's never like that, with us. Our marriage comes first, neither of us would think of doing anything to threaten it. Edwin feels I'm more emotional . . ."

"Well, perhaps he's right."

"And then, it's so good for us, in bed," she went on demurely. "I really don't have much appetite for anyone else."

"I really must be going," I said, and went to call the children.

Flora shouted after me, "Don't forget! I need a dozen eggs for breakfast." We had an agreement.

Jeff complained all the way home. "We didn't stay any time at all! You made us leave too soon! Saul and I were going to look for mushrooms when he came back from fishing."

"I'm sorry," I said, unfeelingly, and turned up the radio to block further complaints. The children's voices continued to nag for my attention but I was able to maintain my separateness by thinking of Mary Cassaday's party, imagining what Edwin would do there, what he would say, how he would look, and planning to snatch a few minutes alone with him.

Driving up to our house, I saw David raking the leaves near the porch. He waved. "Did you have a good time?" he called pleasantly as I stepped out of the car. I was annoyed by his useful compliance: my friends had automatically become his friends, my family had replaced his family, and now it seemed that my love affair, too, was becoming his—a source of vitality and vicarious excitement. "Why should I have had a good time?" I asked, passing him rapidly. "I only went there to pick up the children."

"Was everybody there?"

"No, only Flora." Grudgingly, I added, "The rest had gone off fishing."

"If I had known it was only going to be Flora . . ." I went into the house before he could complete his customary compliment. He liked Flora, and would have been pleased if we had all thought that they were having "a thing."

The afternoon passed with the usual procession of obligations. I tracked down the bottled-gasman, who hummed away around the house, hauling out the old cannister and putting in another. Then he waited silently, just inside the kitchen door, while I wrote out his tiny check. Handing it to him, I watched him fold it carefully and store it in his shirt pocket.

David sat down at the kitchen table to read his newspaper; he asked me to make him a cup of tea. I clanked the pot onto the burner. "Why don't you ever pay for anything?" I asked him suddenly.

David widened hiis eyes. "But I do, you know. Theater tickets, dinners out, the payments on the car—"

"I pay every bill that comes into the house."

"My salary doesn't go too far," he said humbly. "I haven't had a new suit in two years."

"But you make a lot of money!" The amount, in fact, had never been clear to me; it varied, and was distributed at odd times. "What is your salary, actually?"

"Well, you know, I've explained it to you—it varies. You don't remember, but we've been over all this before. The partnership agreement stipulates . . . Not till the end of the year." As he expected, I had lost sentences of incomprehensible detail, between.

"Could you write your income down on a piece of paper?" I asked.

"Of course, but it wouldn't make sense to you. It would even be misleading. I mean, the amount might seem large, but when you finish deducting—"

"Subtract the deductions first, then."

"I'll do it for you, next week. I have all those figures at the office."

I subsided. It was part of our silent agreement never to push a conversation to its limit. I knew there was something hidden inside David's bland explanations, but as long as I continued to have enough money of my own to run the household, I preferred to savor my resentment rather than to force him to reveal what might turn out to be only a shabby truth.

The dividends from my trust funds were large and I squandered them guiltlessly, paying taxes and tuition, medical bills and department store charges with the same vague, savorless abandon. I sometimes wondered why I did not enjoy my extravagance more, and remembered shopping as a child in the dimestore with my nurse, delighted to find a ten cent book of paper dolls. In the last year, my checking account had been overdrawn twice, and in a small panic, I had raised two loans, using my shares for collateral. David had watched this maneuver from afar, assuring me that actually there was enough money; it was simply a question of cash flow. That did not entirely satisfy me. It had begun to dawn on me as I sat sweating in the bank manager's office that something was finally going wrong. Our magic was running out.

I had grown up in the midst of such smooth and silent manifestations of wealth that the slightest financial deprivation seemed unimaginable, vulgar, like a fart at a symphony concert. My parents had used their money to compensate for other disappointments. I never cried as a child when they went away because I knew they would come back loaded with Greek dolls, English coins, even the costumes of exotic lands for me to parade in. On birthdays and Christmases, the stacks of presents towered, sometimes badly-chosen or inappropriate but always so beautiful, so expensive that it did not seem possible to complain. Their presents were redolent of the world outside; they only shopped in New York, London or Paris. Later, when no one danced with me at parties because I was tall and cheerless and too bright, my mother bought me boxes full of pastel dresses, elaborately trimmed. I was certainly the best-dressed scarecrow at the party. It mattered. It made up, a little. More important, it taught me to depend on money as an infallible source of small satisfactions when the other sources consistently, regularly dried up.

Irritated, I poured David's tea. "You never have even paid for the boys' tuition," I complained. I realized that I was on the verge of a vile accusation.

"Maybe I can help you with the tuition next year," David said.

I hardly heard him. A vile accusation: it is not the same thing to grudge money and to grudge sex. To my horror, I had made the connection. I began to slice up onions and carrots to make my soup. Still the words repeated themselves: David gives me nothing. The knife chopped the carrot neatly. He gives me nothing.

Half an hour later, I was stirring the soup and still repelling the invasion of that dishonest accusation. After all, I had always been dry, myself. I had hoped, or depended, at least, on David's orgasm to make up for my lack, to fill me. Now I could turn and turn on his spit but nothing would ever happen to me, or him. Since it did not matter to David, it had seemed for a long time that it should not matter to me. David treated fucking as another not-unpleasant obligation, a way of setting his thumbprint in my flesh. To play at it, to grow angry or ardent, to give abundantly would have been as foreign to him as handing me a great gross handful of jingling change and fluttering ten-dollar bills.

At six, Mrs. T. the babysitter arrived, looming large in the doorway in her scarf and coat; she took off all her layers, then sat at the kitchen table to give me the week's gossip. The lightbulb burned above our heads and the children argued on the stairs while she told me about her brother's disloyalty, the pecuniary malpractices of the telephone company and the probable fate of the proposed Grand Union. Meanwhile Jeff and Keith began to fence in the living room with a pair of plastic swords. Molly settled herself on the couch, the cat in her arms, and began to croon and smooth it. Used to her sudden changes, the cat arched against her arms. "I must go up and dress," I told Mrs. T.

"Why, yes, go right away," she said, chagrined because she had not yet unloaded all her wares. She followed me into the living room and hissed, "Scat!" at the cat. Melvin leaped out of Molly's arms. "Dirty thing!" Mrs. T.'s voice sawed across my daughter's complaint.

Upstairs, I plunged into my ritual. Drawing a bath, I poured in capfuls of sweet oil; the dinner party gave me an excuse to pamper myself. I knew that in the other house, three miles away, Flora would be getting ready, and I imagined Edwin in the bathroom with her, and perhaps even sharing her tub. I lay alone in my tub with my jealousy, my rubber duck. I was determined to believe that Edwin did not love Flora because he did not seem to enjoy her company. Gradually I was beginning to realize that whether he loved her or not was irrelevant. They were fused together. His opinions faded into hers without a seam, they arrived at the same conclusions from different points, or else they disagreed in silence, keeping up the tone. Edwin's impressions seemed to have been filtered through the blue glass of Flora's moralizing; he could only enjoy himself around its edges. Since Flora permitted his badness, the circle they formed could not be broken by discontent. Love, after all, is a luxury compared to the addiction of mutual dependence. I got out of the bath, dried off, and pulled on my stockings.

David was already dressed and shaved, having used the downstairs bathroom. We avoided seeing each other naked. Six months of abstinence had made us both unusually polite. David arranged himself to conform to my unspoken demands, dressed and undressed apart from me and slid into bed beside me as apologetically as a stranger. I knew he hoped I would continue to put up with him as long as he continued to put up with me.

We went downstairs. The children were eating their supper in the kitchen in brutalized silence. They had offended Mrs. T., who was clashing pots in the sink. She made a face at me and shrugged at Jeff, who was crying into his soup. I could not afford to inquire into the trouble, which might cloud or even forestall my plesaure in the evening. I hacked off a slice of bread, buttered it lumpily and offered it to Jeff. He pushed it away. "I hate dark bread." I kissed each one of their resisting faces; David kissed them, too, and we walked out of the house together.

A starry night: I took his arm, reminded of the nights of our first autumn in the country. After a day spent taking care of children, we would walk a little way down the dark road, afraid to be gone for more than a few minutes, holding each other's hands. Pleased by my touch, David announced, "I thought it was a very nice day."

"Yes."

"A little hectic, as always, but the children had a good time."

"Yes."

"Molly seems to be coming down with a cold."

"So it seems."

We got into the car. David started the motor and negotiated the front gate. Snapping on the radio, I flooded the car with the ridiculous songs which had become my panacea and my revenge. David turned the volume very slightly down. "Do you mind?"

"Not at all."

There is a point in a marriage beyond which the only hope lies in silence—total, smooth and entirely accepted silence, a wax over the unknown.

We were fixed in our separate worlds by the time we reached the bright glass house, ten miles up the river in the little town of Ransom. Light streamed out of the walls and roof of the house, which was a frame for panels of glass. Hurrying across the bridge to the front door, we were both animated for the first time in days. "That dress is very becoming," David announced.

"You don't think it's too tight?"

"Not since you lost weight."

Mary Cassady welcomed us with open arms. Her beautiful delicate face was decorated with thread-like lines; it seemed that they would drift off any minute and leave her face smooth again. In a husky whisper, she directed me myteriously to lay my shawl upstairs. Mary was full of secrets and suppositions, turning the dreariest country evening into a field for intrigue. I loved her imagination and often asked her to repeat stories about the people we knew, stories which were always more thrilling than anything reality offered, or to describe the days when her children were small and she turned them out into the snow, in desperation, to work on a poem.

Upstairs, I laid down my shawl and wondered what Flora would think when she saw it. She disliked the brightness of my clothes and might well cover my red shawl with her beige one. Then I remembered that I had forgotten to bring her the eggs. I was frightened. It was the first time I had neglected to bring her tribute.

I stood for a minute by the window, listening to the stream that curled around the foundations of the house. The country sound swelled and filled my attention and I was for a while relieved. I smiled, looking at the double bed, and entertained the vision of the four of us—David, and me, and Flora and Edwin—sitting up as straight as dolls against the plump pillows. Perhaps after all that was what we wanted: a family, erotically entwined. The relief of laughing made me generous, and I understood for the first time how Edwin could lose himself talking to his patients or chopping wood, lose himself more effectively than he even lost himself with me, for with me, guilt admitted a pinpoint of light.

I arrived on the stairs in time to receive them. Flora, the cake huddled in her arms, was wearing her old red corduroy skirt. Edwin had put on the wrinkled prep-school blazer and shrunken white pants which made him look like the ill-fated captain of a mutinous ship. He snatched Mary Cassady into his arms, kissed her ear and hugged her firmly, rocking her back and forth; she fell in with the motion. I went down the stairs. When the time came, I held out my hand; Edwin took it, startled. Then I hugged and kissed Flora, with little cries.

Without a word, Edwin turned towards the living room and I followed, mastering my panic, chattering to Flora. "I'm sorry about the eggs. . ." She looked at me with enormous irritation. "It simply means Edwin won't have eggs for breakfast." I left her to make the round of the little circle of friends, standing near the fire. Helena greeted me with an exclamation of pleasure, holding me off to admire my dress. "I've been calling you all week!" she said. "We really must talk," and she looked at me with a surmise which frightened me. "What have you—?" I began but Charles came over and slipped his arm around my waist. "The prettiest girl at the party." We were all in line again.

Winty Cassaday made my drink and brought it without a word. Hooded in his reserve, he took up his post beside the fire. He was the only person I did not dare to kiss. Frugal, hard-working, he was not a weekend visitor but a fulltime country schoolteacher. He had served the local high school for thirty years, which everyone said was a waste and an example of his lack of self-confidence; he had a degree in Philosophy from Harvard. Winty had no theory about education; he simply liked to live in the country. At parties, Winty was never talkative or drunk or flirtatious but simply, totally removed. Mary was his only vice, apparently. The summer before, I had walked with him in Mrs. Lyton's rose garden, crying because Edwin had not been to see me for a month. "You should leave him," Winty had remarked at the end of our promenade, and I realized that he had mistaken me for Flora.

Parker Harris drew me to his side. "You are looking simply marvelous, as always; what a smashing dress." The compliment was not undone by his irony. Parker was a slight, dapper man with a blond moustache; his eyes were very bright. We began to talk and laugh together—Parker with his sense of style would never let me complain. He lent tone to my life, to all our lives, which he seemed to see objectively, in a glassy blue glare, as though lit from above by a fluorescent tube. Eddy Lang, Parker's friend, who rumor claimed had supplied all the money for the big house they had bought at Long Wharf, came up and kissed my hand. I was delighted by the attention. His lips on the back of my hand seemed real compared to the feel of my own lips on everyone else's cheeks. He began to tease me about my long hair, which I had been threatening to cut. "I see you are still hoping to draw up a prince." Parker and Eddy both disliked Edwin, whom they accused of being irresponsible; Parker and Eddy were both careful, even cautious in their dealings, sensitive to the slightest swing in mood or opinion in the people around them. The local gentry, the river folk, scorned them for basing their lives on sexual preference; in spite of their charm, they fell into the same category as the millionaire who had installed his mistress in one of the river places. Parker and Eddy did not ignore the slights, the turned backs at the supermarket, the invitations ostentatiously ignored, the fawning friendliness when a new piece of upholstery or an extra man was needed. They were not bitter. They often seemed quite gleeful at the sight of the discomfort they caused. They were an idea whose time would never come, and they had been unfailingly kind to me.

Looking at their trim small bodies, I wondered if they took pleasure in each other, in spite of Parker's waspishness and Eddy's bad back, or whether they had settled, like the rest of us, for the voyeurism of middle age.

Mary Cassaday was lighting candles in the dining room and calling us in a whispery yet penetrating voice. As we went in, I saw our reflections, as white as ghosts, in the long windows behind the dinner table. Mary seated us according to a written plan. I was on Edwin's left. Too lucky: I knew it at once. Edwin did not look at me or pull out my chair. We were made for difficulties, after all, not for the obscenely smooth working of a benign fate.

Edwin sat down and turned immediately to Ellen Cassaday, Mary's eldest daughter, who was seated on his right. I was frightened. What had I done? Then I remembered the moment on the stairs. I turned hastily to Eddy, on my right, and launched into conversation. His brown eyes were dead and I wondered what kind of hell Parker had made of his day. I asked him about his sister. Eddy was the pillar of a large, tottering family. He gave them money, which they accepted, and advice which they invariably ignored. He sent them to colleges, and other institutions, shaken by their failures but never in despair. "Lou-lou has gone out West to take the cure," he told me; "This time she seems really to want to change." He went on to say that he was running out of money; his small advertising firm had been hit hard by the recession and he did not know, anymore, whether or not he would be able to send his youngest niece to college.

I listened to Eddy with difficulty, through a numbing clang. Edwin had turned sideways in his chair to enchant Ellen. His back, broad as a wall, was set in my face. I reminded myself that he did not go after young women; their expectations were too high. As I heard pretty Ellen Cassaday laughing, I remembered Edwin's fascination with mothers and daughters. Certainly at some point in the last five years, he had fucked Mary, behind a sofa, at a party, behind a tree; to get into her daughter would cap the memory and prove, as well, that he was appreciated—his medicine effective in both generations. I was beginning to feel sick. I could not eat. Where was the gentleness, which I mistook for love, when he first touched me in the wet field, a year ago? I thought then we were alone together. Now we seemed only to exist in terms of our effect on others. I had become Edwin's tool, his weapon in the longdrawn silent battle with his wife. "You don't know what he's like," Flora had called after me, a year ago, a lifetime ago, when I started out with Edwin to pick wild grapes for jelly. Our first public escapade—and we made plans, then, for more. Flora and Edwin had drawn up a contract which allowed for his fucking and her bad temper; both were meaningless extravagances. I did not believe it, then. I could not believe it until the words of the contract had been carved in my bones.

Eddy was talking steadily, softly, trying to find my attention. Knowing that something was wrong, he was offering me a picnic, a night at the races, a chance to taste a new white wine. I accepted all his invitations, ducking my head, afraid to trust my voice. "Nobody believes in goodness anymore," Flora announced stridently, across the table; she was trying to work up an argument with Winty, who was known to go to church on Sundays. I heard everything she said at my outer edges, preoccupied with my own contract with Edwin, that sunsigned, sunsealed promise we made in the grape-arbor: no marriages and no divorces. I had laughed then, seeming to agree, tossing my head, unable to believe that the delightful flirtation would harden into genuine slavery.

Suddenly Edwin turned to me. He did not look at me as he began to talk. "Mary shouldn't have put us together. It was a mistake. You see, it isn't fun, anymore."

I was silenced, pain undoing rage.

He went on, "There are three types of schizophrenics. One shatters like a glass. One dents like celluloid and fills out again. The third doesn't break or dent. It gives off a tin clang. Do you know which kind you are?"

That was because I wore the tight white dress.

"You are the third kind."

I turned my head on its hinge and asked Eddy about his other niece, the older one. He told me she had slashed her wrists on Labor Day weekend when her parents were away and she was in the house alone. He was horrified by their negligence; the girl had nearly died. Tears were filling my eyes. They crawled slowly down my cheeks, which were so hot the tears dried at once. Eddy glanced at me and took a sip of wine. "Excuse yourself," he said.

I left the table, with a clatter, knocking off my knife. Edwin had turned his back and was laughing with Ellen. I saw David across the table, staring at me. With my napkin balled in my fist, I went upstairs.

Mary's bathroom was cold; a window was opened. I sat on the toilet lid, in the dark, slit by a triangle of light from the open door. Their voices came up the stairwell. I stuffed part of the napkin in my mouth. We fell into bed together, the last time—a sunny Wednesday. I licked Edwin down his chest and up again, taking his fresh balls in my mouth. We had not agreed to such intimacy. Later he came in my mouth and I swallowed his sperm, loving what he gave me. It was too much. It was always too much, after the first furtive fucking.

I had never seen the smile I had seen on his face after he had fucked somebody's wife during the second half of a country concert; he came out of the men's room just in time to drive Flora home, and he was beaming.

I knew all that about him. I was not deceived. For five years, Flora had been providing me with the details. She was proud of him and exasperated by him about equally. Yet I still felt that his smooth cock erecting between my thighs meant love. His absence, his torture, felt like love to me, the real thing, pain and pleasure unequally mixed. The absence of decency meant honesty, the absence of warmth meant truth, the perpetual threat of rejection meant that we were working on each other like yeast, rising to new heights of perception and pain. I wanted to suck his little nipples and claim him for my own because he was unclaimable, a scourge of God, a gift of love.

Finally I turned on the bathroom light and brushed my hair with Mary's silver-backed brush and washed the tear-scabs off my cheeks. Then I started down the stairs in my beautiful white dress which was too well-fitted, too flattering. Eddy was waiting for me at the bottom.

"All right?"

"Yes."

We went into the living room.

# 10.

It is almost ten o'clock and the cars are arriving steadily. Jeff and Molly are outside directing parking. Molly flashes into the house. "Eleven cars and more coming! Should they park by the barn? They must!" she shouts. "The place by the shed is all full." It is a feast, a festival—friendly strangers arriving in their cars on this warm, high-skied day. The shadows are short, now, the grass has dried, and the sun is hot without the sting of August. This day is the fruit of my planning and my perseverence; I am determined to enjoy it. Snatching at Molly as she flies by, I ask, "The Fields—where are they sitting?"

She deflates suddenly, comes to a dead standstill. "At the back. Saul wouldn't say hello to me." She is off at once, wriggling out of my grip. I fight hard for a minute against the rage her rejection inspires and then suddenly I let the rage flood me. They shall not continue to make my children suffer. (We shall not continue to make their children suffer?) We have not spoken to each other publicly since Easter. Yet the children continue to ask to see each other, and occasionally they succeed.

They are acting, it seems to me, not out of innocence or confusion but on the faith in good intentions and continuing relationships which we, their parents, have been unable to take from them. They act on our ideals, having somehow failed to see that the ideals fell like dead leaves in the first wind.

Our public connection, the old solid link between our two families, forged out of so many weekends and holidays spent together, collapsed when I asked Edwin to leave Flora and come to me. That was in the spring, at the peak of my hope and its matched despair when Edwin, hard-pressed at last by feelings he didn't want, was trying every way he could find to reject me without words, and I was trying every way I could find to hold on. I decided that he should know that my intentions were honorable: I wanted him. Edwin refused me, in a frozen rage. My proposition proved that I understood nothing about him. I was blinded by my own need. How could I have imagined that because we pleased each other so much, he would leave Flora for me? The two things, in Edwin's mind, were not connected; there was no valid comparison. My request travelled fast along our subcutaneous system, never discussed yet immediately absorbed; Flora knew in a day, David in a week. No one mentioned what had happened, of course, but we all began, at once, to avoid each other. The words for change, I realize now, inspire as much terror as change itself. Meanwhile our children continue to telephone each other and to arrange visits; one parent or another drops them off at the gate. They appear as though by providential magic, borne on the breeze.

I began to telephone Edwin, after he refused me; I telephoned him at his office every day, every week, sweating with shame and anxiety. I had to change my clothes, afterwards, to get rid of the sour stink of fear. I gave businesslike messages to his answering service—how knowing their voices sounded—or, on bad days, hung up in terror when those ladies answered. Edwin did not return my calls, no matter how I worded the message. There was no way to root him out of his lair. Finally I began to write him letters, which I hope I will never have to read. Pleading, explaining—he did not answer them, either. In the country, I sometimes drove by their house and saw the smoke drifting out of the chimney and the dog nosing around the geraniums and the children's bikes sprawled on the grass: the daily routine continuing unaltered by my anguish. It seemed a miracle to me, a profound mystery of uncaring—that they could eat and sleep and continue untouched by my despair. Edwin would not see me, alone, and I would not descend to tracking him down, in the supermarket, in the midst of his wife and children. My rage in the end became all I had to offer and I wanted to force him to accept it—but he was afraid, he hid, he refused.

Now the warmth of my rage does not subside: it is with me day and night. It is a spark, a little fire, newly kindled; I keep it going with my breath.

I notice David standing in the shadow by the living room window, watching people arrive. "It looks like a big crowd," I say to him, inspired by the warmth of my anger to imitate the old colorless friendly exchanges which have taken up so much of our lives. His good nature and my patience have kept us together for four or five years after the death of hope, the death of the marriage. Now I need him, my fellow conspirator, my confrère peering through the window at the scene outside. I go on, "Molly says the Fields are sitting in the back. Saul wouldn't say hello to her."

David inches his head forward. "Coming here takes some nerve."

"I suppose they want a souvenir, a plate, or something, to show for all those Thanksgivings and Christmases and Saturday nights together."

"Maybe they just came, you know, on their way back from town." He goes on, hurriedly, "I see Mary Cassaday and Eddy and Parker have arrived."

"Good! I mentioned it to all of them but I wasn't sure they'd come. I thought embarrassment might hold them back."

"Embarrassment?"

"Picking over the relics. Some people might be ashamed. I see Helena in front but I don't see Charles."

"You said you wanted them all to come."

"Yes, but there's still the question of embarrassment."

"Yours?"

"I'm long past that."

He looks away. I continue to peer out of the window. The tent is open on this side, its flaps propped up, and I can see rows of rickety church-supper chairs. About half of them are occupied. Mrs. Pultz, the checker at the Grand Union, sits alone in the front row, as imposing as a duchess, an enormous pocketbook clasped in her lap. The Knoors, a tiny old couple who run the antique shop on the highway, are sitting apologetically on the edges of their chairs. They are worrying that I will think they have come to buy things for their shop, which of course they have. I wish them good bargains. Our children used to drop by the little antique store and handle everything and ask for oddments, old nails. Goldsmith, who hayed our fields, is sitting in the middle, wearing his grey sweat-stained fatigues, next to an improbably pretty wife and a row of squirming children. George, the handsome cripple from the gas station—I am surprised to see him, I did not think he knew our name. He is looking across the aisle at Helena, who is wearing her best bluejean jacket with the daisies on the lapels. Parker and Eddy are further down, as discreet as a pair of mice, their hands folded on their laps. Winty has not come. Mary Cassaday's face is strangely severe; I have never seen it before without its decoration of smiles.

I am pleased by the size of the crowd: more are coming. It seems to me that they have come here to honor me as well as to pick over my possessions. Their presence means that there is something of mine which they wish to keep after I am gone and the house is sold. Like a funeral, the auction has a strange cheer; the survivors can never quite disguise their satisfaction. I wonder what ornament or piece of furniture each of these people will choose, and imagine them saying, years from now, "Yes, that came from those city people who had to leave, the ones who had the house on Primrose Hill." It is a form of immortality, a low form, admittedly, but I am not one to quibble. The warmth of my anger makes me generous; I hope they will choose well and go home satisfied.

Tom has climbed onto the front steps and is holding up a pair of David's prints—two views from West Point. His gargling auctioneer's voice fills the room. "Five? Do I hear five? Five? Five? All right, we'll start at three-fifty."

"I'm not going to lurk in here all morning," I tell David. If there was a mountain to climb or a sea to swim, I might be dissuaded, but I cannot hang indoors any longer. Outside, they will think that I'm afraid.

He looks at me sideways, dubiously. "I don't think you ought to go out there."

"I need to go out there, I need to see what those people choose."

He shrugs. "Well, then, go."

I equivocate. "I'm curious to see what they think our things are worth."

He says heavily, "Curiosity seekers. They probably won't even bid."

"Oh no, they want to take something home, I'm sure of that." Still, I hesitate. Fred bangs in.

"We need some small things, to get them started," he says, a little feverish himself. Glancing around the room, he notices the silver candlesticks on the mantel and reaches for them. David stretches out his hand. "Not those."

"She said—" Fred stops at the look on David's face, a terrible look, as though he is guarding his only child.

"Not your grandmother's candlesticks," David tells me, glaring.

"I don't want them anymore."

"For the children."

"They don't care about those candlesticks. They never even knew her. I know they mean a lot to you—they're very fine." David in fact has looked them up in one of his silvermark books. He is delighted by everything that is rare or old, as though it proves the authenticity of its owners. "If you want them, you can bid on them when they come up."

Fred backs off hastily and snatches up an inoffensive blue pottery bowl on his way out.

"I'm not going to bid for those candlesticks." For the first time, David is implacable: he has been touched.

He reaches for them. I put my hand between them and his hand, and my hand, as small and dry as a leaf, stops him. He will not descend to force although he may be tempted. "I told you I wouldn't let you take anything at the last minute. I need every penny I can get. Besides, it wouldn't be fair to Tom," I explain.

"I don't care about that. You're selling everything. You're selling the past."

"If it was possible—that's what I wanted to do."

"Adolescent," he snaps.

"Yes. I want to be wanted for myself, I want to be wanted for my hands and my arms and my legs and my face and whatever there is inside me. Just like a teenager stripped in front of a mirror. The way Edwin wanted me, once, for five minutes—just me, bare, without any decoration. The way you never wanted me, even at the start. You wanted what I stood for and I put up with that: a pair of beautiful old Georgian silver candlesticks. Sterling, at that. There is something else. There is something entirely different. You never wanted that."

"Don't be ridiculous, I love you, I always have, I am very proud of you."

"Yes, I made a handsome decoration, trailing money, possessions, relatives."

"Believe what you want to believe. It has nothing to do with those candlesticks."

I take hold of one smooth cold stick, lift it down from the mantel and reach for the other. "I used to think you married me for my money but now I know it was a purer snobbery. Great-grandfather's letters from the battle of Bull Run, Grandfather's Legin of Honor, Grandmother's stories of the old days—all so laughable, so desirable. I could have understood that, if you had told me; it was tripping and falling over it in the dark that hurt."

"I want Molly and Jeff," he says suddenly.

I do not understand him; I look charming and baffled.

"I want Molly and Jeff," he repeats.

In panic, I laugh and push the candlesticks in his direction. "Here. You can have them."

"I don't want them," he says, his voice smooth as he tastes my fear. "I have plenty of that kind of thing."

I master my panic, the mother climbing my throat. "You have Keith—we agreed on that. You can't have Molly and Jeff. It's just not possible—you know that."

"I believe they would be better off with me."

"That's a strange thought, at this moment. You never wanted them before." Yet I am rapt with curiosity; I wonder what he thinks would be better for them, and why.

"I'm thinking of their best interest," he says.

"I won't permit it, David. It's unthinkable."

"My lawyer thinks I have a fairly strong case," he says, conversationally.

"I know you've been gathering evidence—that's the yellow pad. Shit, Bastard," I say, meditatively. "Here in my own house, under my own roof."

"It is our house," he says.

"Was it ever? You never made a fire here, or cooked a meal here, or got up in the night with a child. You never made me come with you, in bed."

"I paid the mortgage installments," he says dryly. "The other things, I might have done as well."

"If what—?"

"You never made it easy for me, Ann. You jumped to do everything yourself. With the children, especially. You never made me feel it mattered what I did, or didn't do. The children felt that, too. You erased me."

"Erase me, you unerasable you," I sing, my mad inappropriate humor spreading like a sail.

"And then, with Edwin. Even the children knew what was going on. Locking yourself in the guest room with him, the day after Thanksgiving, with the children in the next room. You haven't been very careful."

"No court is going to declare me an unfit mother."

"That isn't necesssary, anymore. They may ask the children what they want. Their opinions, at least, will be taken into account. And what I can offer them."

"All the money you saved from the years when I was paying."

"I don't mean money," he says with dignity.

"But the money will mean something. The money you saved will buy them what I can't afford to buy them now— vacations, a handsome apartment, all the lovely little extras. You'll niggle and niggle on child support but if they were living with you, you would give them everything, and a judge will know that."

"The only thing that really matters is what the children want," he says with a lofty assurance which terrifies me.

I think of Molly's perpetual whining, Jeff's dim small frown. "You'll destroy them. Why don't you beat me, instead, tear me limb from limb—"

He rears back. "I don't want to hurt you. I never have. I've never been angry at you. I know you simply couldn't help yourself. I just believe the children will be happier with me. They're going to need stability, routine. You said yourself you were going to change your life. You said you might want to travel."

"What has that got to do with it?"

David waits while Fred comes in and goes out with a carton of books.

"It has a lot to do with it. They need security. I want them to live in one place, quietly, with a good housekeeper, friends, school, a calm emotional atmosphere."

"And you can provide all that?"

"I can try."

"You're talking like a Daddy at last."

"They won't have that, with you. Your emotional swings were hard enough for them to take, before, when I was around and the situation was normal. Now they'll be entirely exposed to your bad temper, your depressions. Think of them. Ann, not just yourself."

I move to stand six inches in front of him. He averts his eyes, leaving his fixed face for me to stare at. "I'm not crazy, David. You'll never convince anyone of that." The word, released in the room, flutters its wings.

"No one is thinking about that. No one is trying to prove anything." Yet the word is there, vigorous, with a life of its own.

"That's a lie, and you know it. You are going to try to prove that I'm incompetent. That was always your way of dealing with me: explain my feelings away as some kind of aberration. What you don't understand is labeled and put outside the pale." I do not add that he has half-convinced me.

"All that is in the past, now," he says.

"Yes, but it's on the past, or on your version of the past that you're acting. It won't do, David. What's more, it won't work. You can't have Molly and Jeff."

"You never should have told me about Edwin," he says calmly. "You exposed yourself."

"You and I were trying to work things out then! We were trying to be honest, and humane—to understand. It hadn't become a question of judgments, yet. We weren't enemies, we weren't storing up ammunition—"

"Still, you exposed yourself."

"But you condoned it."

"Not legally. And besides, that has nothing to do with the welfare of the children. I've given it a lot of thought, Ann, and I'm determined to save them."

"From me!"

"You can see them whenever you want."

Molly runs in. "Eric from riding school is here. Can I take out some of the peanut butter cookies?"

"Go ahead," I tell her. My mouth is dry.

Stalling for time, I turn my back on David and watch my daughter dart into the kitchen. All my little ones. Surely the months I carried them in my belly and the pain of their births must count for something; the months I spent nursing them, the interminable procession of interrupted nights. David had nothing to do with their beginnings, after the moment of conception; the babies existed in the remote reaches of his imagination, if at all—little candles on the altar of his manhood. Who will care? What does it matter? Even I didn't care, at the time. He left me alone at the feast.

"Eric might want something to drink," Molly says, flying by with the cookies.

David goes on, "Ann, believe it or not, I'm trying to spare you. I'm not telling you things I feel you can't tolerate. Just the broad outlines. I don't want to upset you, I know how hard this is for you. But believe me, it will be best for everyone in the long run. You'll be able to have your own life—"

"I have my own life. My life is not something you can give me, or take away."

"You'll have your independence. I know how much that has always meant to you. And the children will have a stable home to grow up in."

"Go to hell. Go to hell, you bastard, you stinking shit."

"If you wanted to keep the children, you should have behaved differently. You should have been more careful. You could have avoided allowing them to see you with Edwin—"

"They never saw me!"

"I don't mean actually in bed," he says, dryly. "They were certainly parties to your intimacy."

"They loved it. The meals and the days we had together. The best fun of their lives."

David clasps his hands. They are trembling as he wards off the great blow of his rage. "You let them know exactly what was happening. That was why Keith couldn't stand the idea of living with you, without me. He thought it would be more of the same."

"So that is what you two have been discussing."

"I answered his questions, Ann. I couldn't very well avoid them."

"You could have told me, at least."

"I didn't want to upset you," he says.

"I won't accept that. I won't accept your version of the truth, or your kindness. You've taken Keith, for vengeance, and now you want to take the others, for the same reason— to break me. It has nothing to do with the children or their welfare. It has to do with your rage. You've seen me growing stronger since you moved out, since you stopped living on me, and now you want to punish me for that, to break me by taking my children.

"Be quiet, Ann, they'll hear you."

In the silence, I hear Tom's voice, drumming outside the window.

"You can't have them," I say. I am suddenly so tired my eyelids ache.

"We'll see about that." He makes a bracket with his hands, enclosing the case. "My lawyer will be in touch with yours next week. You made your choice, Ann, you made it a long time ago, whether you knew it or not."

He turns away. Watching him, I feel the pull towards despair, the vacuum opening in front of me. David's assurance will win the case before he even needs to make use of his evidence. I see myself snivelling in the dock, a bad mother, a self-confessed adulteress. "Yes, your honor, I did neglect my children. I did give them peanut butter to eat out of the jar while my lover and I went and fucked like little dogs."

Raging at my complicity, I shout after David, "I'm going to fight you on this one, I'm going to fight you and you are not going to win."

He disappears into the parlor.

I rush into the kitchen, bang through cabinets, open the refrigerator. The smooth handles of my secret storage places reassure me. I stand looking into the bright empty refrigerator, remembering when it was crowded with food, remembering its little light at two in the morning, after everyone had gone home. Surely such innocent joys, such touching and kissing cannot lead to this catastrophe. We were not innocent yet our desire for each other had the strength of innocence— Edwin and I snatching each other as my babies once snatched my breast. Need is all—and yet it has come to this, to this punishment, this destruction, this final assault of pain.

I know the edge of the cloud is very close and advancing rapidly towards me. One false step and I will be in darkness. I am frightened of my own despair, which is complicity. I remember my weekends alone when the children are with David; I remember lying in bed late in the morning, masturbating, the sun flowing in through the window, I remember the obscure and permanent pleasure of my self-sufficiency, coming for my own hand as I never came for a man. Life in the desert.

The children are not my life but they are my ties to the world, the channels through which my energy runs. Without them, I will lose my sense of myself as a functioning human being, a needed woman, a supplier of hope and love. I must keep my place in the world if I am to survive; otherwise I will lapse into the solitariness of my childhood. Then, there was always an escape—there was growing up. This time there will be no escape.

I must act, I must find a way to lay my hand on the day, the massed heavy day which started out as a will-o'-the-wisp, a drifting hope, a triumph. Now I must somehow twist or bend this heavy shape to what is left of my will. Staring into the refrigerator, I see four bottles of champagne, lying side by side on the botttom shelf. They have been lying there since my birthday, in August, which I did not celebrate because we had no friends.

I say outloud, in a piercing girlish tone, the tone of gaiety, induced, forced, "We are going to drink this champagne!" I expect to hear a protest, my children doubting, David doubling himself up to repress his irritation, but the kitchen is large and empty, as empty as it will be tomorrow when we are all gone.

The glasses have been taken away already but there is still a stack of paper cups by the sink. I pile the cups on the tray, arrange the bottles, find a corkscrew in the muddled drawer of leftovers. Then I lift the unwieldy tray and make for the front door. David stares at me with astonishment from his post in the parlor.

"Where are you going with that?"

"I am going to offer our friends some champagne."

He does not say anything else; his arm jerks out, as though it would halt me. "That's very foolish," he breathes as I pass.

I open the front door with one hand, balancing the rattling tray, and step out. Tom's voice is ahead of me on the steps. I edge my way around it. A bottle slides and threatens to fall; I stop and right it. There are rows of faces in front and slightly below me, rows of hands and feet. I do not recognize anyone, now; I am blinkered, staring at my tray. I carry it to the back of the tent where Mrs. Porter has set up her stand, selling coffee and doughnuts. She stares at me through her blue-framed glasses. I set the tray down on the trampled grass.

The Fields are sitting in the last row, directly in front of me. Saul turns, hastily, to catch a glimpse of me, then jerks his head around. Flora, Edwin and the children are sitting in a line, staring straight ahead. I see Flora's heels, in her old sandals. Her heels look crushed and small. Edwin is wearing his sneakers with the holes over the toes. The children's feet perch like birds on the chair rungs.

I begin to unwrap the foil on the top of the first bottle of champagne.

Suddenly Edwin is getting up and climbing across his children's knees. He comes towards me, staring at the side of the tent. I see his face, averted, above me, the deep lines beside his mouth, his pallor, his dead grey eyes. A terrible devastation has been carried out on his face.

He crouches beside me and I see the holes in his sneakers.

"You don't use a corkscrew for champagne."

"You always thought I was so spoiled."

"You always had men to do it for you."

"Let me do it now."

"No. Let me help you," he says, for the first and the last time.

I watch his hands fumbling with the crinkled foil. He is working very slowly and methodically, making his task more complicated. I remember his hands on the chainsaw, his hands setting the logs for the fire, his hands on my thighs, parting me. He lays aside the foil and begins to uncoil the harness of wires underneath. "Will it pop?" he asks.

"Yes, it will pop."

He aims the bottle away from me and pulls the cork. It pops out with a small spurting explosion, causing heads to turn. The champagne foams over his hand. We look at each other, smiling at the memory of our love-making. "An embarrassment of riches," he says. Then he begins to fill a row of paper cups. I set them up, one by one, and he tips the bottle, filling each cup halfway, then twisting the neck of the bottle so that it will not drip as he passes it along to the next. How deft he is, how careful, what healing magic there has always been for me in the sight or the touch of his ministering hands.

"Start passing them," he says and I take a cup and thrust it over Flora's shoulder, aiming at her hand, which is cleanched in her lap.

She jerks her head around, stares at me, then glances at the cups. She, too, has grown older, the lines in her face spreading from a point of pain I can't perceive. "What's this?" she asks, in her familiar tone, rasping, grudging.

"Champagne, or poison."

"Can I have some?" It is Saul, the intractable. I settle one cup in Flora's fingers and hand Saul another.

Flora snatches it from him. She holds the cups over her head, out of his reach.

I give another cup to Frank, who takes it without a word. Then I go back to Edwin. He has filled more cups now and is about to open the second bottle. I hear the pop as I pass along the rows; smiling, bowing, I am as cautious as a church warden passing the plate. Yet I am giving, not receiving. The country people balk in amazement. I thrust the cups into their hands. I do not see anyone take a sip. It does not matter. They are holding the cups.

On my way back to Edwin, I see Saul snatch his cup from Flora's hand. She begins to whisper to him fiercely. He turns his head away from her in order not to hear and grasps the cup so tightly he crushes its edges. Champagne leaks down his hand; Flora pulls away her knees. "I wanted to try it," he whines and glances at me—I am his excuse for naughtiness now, his link to the unabridged life.

As I begin to pass more cups, I hear Tom auctioning the firescreen where the children hung their Christmas stockings; bidding is sparse. I am distracting attention from Tom, with my darting runs. "This is to celebrate," I say, handing a cup to Mary Cassaday.

"My dear—" Her voice is a despairing sigh.

"I would like some," Parker says next to her, as gently as though he was holding my hand. Eddy stares, bleak and abashed, his advice dried up.

Edwin is pouring from the third bottle when I return. "Do they like it?" he asks.

"They're taking it, at least."

"Good." For the last time, we are conspiring together, playing our game.

I give Helena a cup from the last batch. She takes it with a grimace. "Ann," she whispers, across her staring neighbor, "you must be terribly upset, this is all so difficult, can you have lunch next Tuesday?"

"No more lunches," I tell her, with a smile to take the edge off. "No more feasting on my bones."

"Why Ann, you know perfectly well—"

I turn away. I will miss her, I will miss all of them.

Edwin is pouring from the last bottle. I take cups to Eddy and Parker, my mates, my unmale men, my true friends. The backs of their heads look as neat and as dark as dolls', as though the hair were painted. I bend over them and hand them two cups. "I'm so glad you could come," I say, to make them laugh: a parody of my hostess voice. They look up at me, startled.

"I hope it's not domestic," Parker says with a smile.

"Do you have no faith?" I kiss his soft forehead. "You two have been . . ." I kiss Eddy, at the top of his nose. They both turn their heads slightly away. Mary Cassaday is watching.

I hurry back to Edwin, who is still crouching on the trampled grass, filling the last cups from the last bottle. "That's it," he says.

"You have this cup." I select one, for him.

He takes the paper cup and stands up, unfolding slowly, his thin knees creaking. "A great idea, Ann," he says in his dead voice. The lines beside his mouth are as deep as scars.

"Will you go on again now, the same way?"

"What do you mean?"

"Taking women . . ."

"Edwin." Flora's voice cracks, over the children's heads. He turns. She motions with her hand, sharply beckoning, her face rigid with fear and rage.

"Goodbye," he says, and leans down to set his cup of champagne, untasted, in the center of the tray.

I watch him turn, take a few short steps, hunch himself across his children's knees and settle in the chair next to Flora. He is still and calm as he sinks into his allotted place. She has claimed him. He will never be mine. He was never mine. I never had him, and yet it seemed that I lost him again and again, every time he turned his face away, every time he left me. This is the last time. This is the final loss.

Tom is auctioning the rocker. Frank raises his hand, startling me; he waves it desperately. Flora, her face set dead ahead, seems unaware of what he is doing. Tom catches sight of Frank's hand, hesitates, then accepts his bid. Mrs. Knoor is waving, in the front row, but her funds are quickly exhausted. Frank buys the rocker for twenty-five dollars; I wonder where he will get the money to pay for it. Flora always wanted that rocker. I used to sit in it to sew, beside the fire.

Fred brings the rocker down the aisle and sets it at the end of the Fields' row. It moves gently back and forth on the crushed grass. I realize that I am not prepared for them to buy it; I am not prepared to go that far. The sight of the rocker, beside them, in all its homeliness, is more than I can bear. Words flash against the backdrop of Tom's voice: this time Edwin will not leave me painlessly.

The words pound in my head. I stand up, fathering myself, behind Flora and her family.

Fred comes out of the house with the box of Christmas tree ornaments. He sets it at Tom's feet. Bending, Tom picks out the silver angel which we used to put on the top of the tree.

This time he will not leave me painlessly.

"What am I bid for this box of balls, and things? Some strings of lights. Nice. Nothing broken, as far as I can see."

Saul's hand shoots up.

"No," Flora hisses, batting at his hand, across Edwin. Edwin is still, his face set ahead.

Saul whines, "I want that angel!" His hand is still up, avoiding hers.

"Make him stop!" Flora orders Edwin. He does not move or speak. Flora reaches in front of him to slap at Saul's hand but Tom has already seen him. "Sold for two dollars to the little fellow in the back."

Not painlessly.

I do not want my angel to hang at the top of their tree, I do not want their future built on the ruins of my past.

The warmth of my rage, that little fire all morning building, heats my bones. I walk around the edge of the crowd, leaving the Fields behind. As I look at these people, I see them all dismembered—decent servicable hands, tightly tailored heads floating in the sunny air. They have come to partake of my dismemberment but I will unjoint them, first. The limbs of Edwin's three children float in front of me; Flora's face, stern and pale, drifts by me like a leaf.

Not painlessly, this time.

"I have all sorts of feelings for you," Edwin said once, when we were bathing together. He has slaughtered them all and rendered them down to the thin grease of fear. He will never touch me again because he knows that I know him.

Not painlessly, this time.

When he left me, I threw a plate on the kitchen floor and smashed it. A flying chip cut my palm. The flap of skin healed badly and I will have that tiny scar in the palm of my right hand for the rest of my life. I was always able to please Edwin, but could not hurt him; that was why the pleasure had no value, no weight, no reality, for him—as though it lacked ballast, flimsy and illusory as a cloud, without the pure weight of inflicted pain. Perhaps he would have believed that I loved him if I had been able to hurt him.

I crouch and duck out of the tent, realizing as I bend my head that my neck is stiff to cracking. I walk across the grass towards the covey of cars.

Molly runs up behind me. "Where are you going?"

"For a little drive."

"I want to come. It's boring here."

"Life is boring, Molly. Boring, or painful."

"I want to come with you, anyhow."

"Better not," I say, to myself.

"Why better not?" I do not answer. "Tom's beginning to auction off my stuff—my bed's next, and my table."

She is pleading, and I am sorry for her; I cannot bear to see the bleak droop of her eyes.

"All right, you can come," I say.

She scurries along beside me. As we walk to the car, the air hums with threats. I remember the big summer storms, rolling up the valley from the river, churning the air ahead of them with heavy charges.

"Daddy says he'll buy me a bed with four posts, when I come to live with him," Molly says, running to keep up.

"You are not going to live with him, my pet."

She does not answer, avoiding trouble. She runs ahead of me, ferrets through the cars, shouts when she sees our station wagon. She is sitting very straight in the front seat when I arrive.

"Where are we going?" she asks, bouncing, as though we are starting out on a picnic.

I fasten my seatbelt and twist the key in the ignition. "We're going for a drive. Put on your seatbelt. You must do exactly as I say."

She stares at me. I have never spoken so firmly.

I turn the car onto the highway and pick up speed. The highway is deserted; it is the morning of the holiday and most people have already left for their destinations. I press the accelerator down to the floor and the battered car leaps. Along the road, the trees have turned color, blazing, then fading to dusty reds and browns. There are For Sale signs in another of the old fields. Our own pasture has been sold to a developer; he will put up twenty boxes.

"Where are we going?" Molly asks again. "You're driving terribly fast."

I slow down, and wonder if David has noted my driving habits on his yellow pad: unsafe at any speed.

"Don't worry, I'm not going to wreck us," I tell my daughter and feel her relax beside me, confident as always because of the confidence of my words.

We turn onto the humped tree-hung side road. She looks out of the window and says nothing. She knows now where we are going.

Over the bump which used to make her giggle when she was tiny, strapped in her car seat and bouncing high. The car hangs suspended in the air for a moment and comes down with a wrenching thud. "Daddy says it's bad for the springs," she remarks. She is smiling: my partner in crime.

Fuck Daddy. Fuck all daddies, and their wives.

I drive through the Fields' gate, past the shed where Edwin keeps his car. The door is open. I slide the car inside to evade the neighbor's notice. "You stay here, in the car, with the door closed," I tell Molly and reach across her to roll up the window. "I'll be back in a few minutes."

"What are you going to do?"

"Never mind. I'll be back in a few minutes."

I would like to lock her in but I relent when I see her peaked face; she is frightened enough already. "You stay here," I repeat, with the full weight of my new authority. She sits very still, to impress me, as though welded to her seat.

I slam the door and walk around to the front of the car. Edwin's power mower is standing in the corner, next to his gardening tools. Everything he has touched bears his mark; the smoothly-worn handles are circled with bands of invisible fingerprints. I see the red gasoline can and approach it cautiously, leaning down to lift it by the handle. I sigh with mixed relief: it is nearly full.

Molly is watching me through the car window. I wave at her, then hoist the can and walk out of the shed.

I start down the path towards the house. A little smoke is climbing out of the chimney from Edwin's early-morning fire, left banked against their return. How fragile the house looks, how defenseless and pretty, with its green shutters and border of geraniums; it is like an illustration in a children's book, a house of rabbits. It is all Edwin's handiwork, his magic against change. I see the terrace he laid himself, next to the front door, the flowerbed he dug for Flora, the window boxes he hammered together so that she could have her petunias. They are thriving still, falling over the edges of the boxes in long white and purple sprays.

I walk around to the north side of the house where I am out of sight of the road. The handle of the gasoline can is cutting into my fingers. I set it down on the grass and unscrew the top. Tipping the can, I drench the geraniums growing along the house. Their fleshy leaves do not absorb the gasoline; it spatters, staining the paint. Its acrid smell overcomes the citrus smell of the geraniums blooming in the sun.

I have no matches.

Leaving the gasoline can, I slide open the porch door and step inside. The familiar chaos is underlined by the smell of burnt bacon. Rackets and children's boots are heaped on the floor. I hear the tap dripping on plates in the kitchen sink. The table is covered with the remains of their breakfast, the chairs pushed back as though they all rushed out, on impulse, in the midst of toast and tea. Flora's heart-shaped silver tea strainer is winking in the sun.

I know she keeps her matches in the drawer next to the stove. My hand reaches out as though on the end of a pole and seizes them.

Out through the kitchen where we made fruitcake, three Novembers running, Edwin giving us each a boiled dime to drop into the big bowl of batter: we were all his children then.

Out through the porch; I stumble on Peter's knapsack, bulging with books, and nearly fall.

Down the steps to the gasoline can, very red in the sun.

I tip it up again and soak the leaves and the grass, then lunge the liquid against the side of the house. Gasoline splashes my hands; I wipe them on my jeans. Cool air touches my cheek like a set of fingers and I look up the hill and see the bright trees behind the children's swing. It is a beautiful day.

I open the box of matches, select one and strike it against the strip of sandpaper. The tiny flame flares up and goes out. I strike another.

Molly sounds the car horn.

I protect the flame in my cupped hand and lean down to the gasoline-soaked flowers. Carefully I extend the flame towards the spattered leaves. An edge curls and smokes. I carry the flame to a tuft of dried grass which leans against the side of the house. Edwin, trimming with his shears, missed that one. The soaked beard of grass smokes, smolders and catches. I watch the flame lean towards the wall, which is dark with gasoline stains. Beneath the flame, the paint begins to wrinkle. The grass, heavy with its burden, leans closer and another flame, spurting up a separate stalk, follows the first one onto the wall.

Molly sounds the horn, two short and one long. I watch the first flame feeling for a foothold a little higher up the wall. It finds a blister on the paint and lays hold. The second flame is climbing up behind it. The grass at my feet is crackling and a pungent smoke rises. The first flame climbs the wall at its own pace, reaching for the kitchen window. The window is open; I see Flora's gingham curtains suddenly sucked in. The flame touches the white window frame and turns it brown.

The second flame fans out further down the wall and the paint crackles and sears. The first flame is mounting the window frame, edging it like a vine.

A slow scorching, darkening stain is spreading across the north wall of the house, board by board, beneath the kitchen window.

Molly sounds the horn.

The top of the window frame pops and crackles. The second flame, spreading, reaches up. The first and second flames join together. Together, they race for the top of the house.

My God, it is burning. The house is burning.

# Aftermath

Reader, I did not lose them. For ten years, that was all that mattered: I did not lose Molly and Jeff, or even Keith. He went to live with his father, but he visited. The other two stayed with me.

The day after the fire, I was arrested and charged with a felony: committing arson. The arrest was quick and quiet; no one wanted a scandal, least of all Flora, who feared its implications for Edwin's career, and for the children—all the children. She didn't discriminate.

I hired a local lawyer to replace the hot-shot guy my father had summoned (he appeared—my father—as though by magic, Oz revealed when the curtain is pulled back), and she worked out an arrangement with the D.A.: five years' probation with psychological counseling.

That year New York State replaced the temporary insanity charge with something called extreme emotional disturbance, a change that kept me out of a jail for the criminally insane. Of course I pled guilty.

Their insurance company paid Flora and Edwin full replacement cost of the house, and they immediately began work on a new one, designed by the same contractor who had helped us all at the beginning. My father paid off the insurance company and my trust repaid him, so in the end I bought Edwin's and Flora's new house, which I will never see.

My lawyer stood by me. She did more than that: matched David expert for expert, found the scholars who were writing the first texts about abuse—abuse of women, that is, subtle, varied, not necessarily physical—and read the texts into the court record. David wanted the children to choose, but the judge in her wisdom only consulted Keith, because of his age, and Keith's decision I already understood.

I reconciled myself to paying David a handsome monthly sum, called, to save his pride, maintenance rather than alimony. There is a link: I paid in a coin worth as much as the smell of the children's necks after they've been asleep.

I agreed to see a psychiatrist four times a week for a year, at my own considerable expense. He dove with me deep into a dark pool. The waters closed over our heads. Of these bones are coral made: but for a long time I only saw the bones, flashing at me—wishes I'd long nursed for a quick and easy end. The doctor held my hand in the deep cold water, and gradually, gradually, we made our way to the surface. There I saw—what? A bit of flotsam: a child's black patent-leather shoe, a red handkerchief, my own sobs and dreams floating, crimson petals on the dark.

That was my task: acceptance of the bright and foolish virgin, the one who burned all her oil.

For ten years my children cried, or were silent. My daughter's face especially was pale and closed. When it comes to pain, they have learned their lesson. I saw them looking off sometimes, or sitting quietly—that was rare—or paging through a book or flipping the channels on TV, and I knew they were back in the house in the country. "Someday they will understand"—another foolish circumlocution. Someday they will understand.

Does this mean we all forgive each other? Who knows? Now that I live alone—Jeff and Molly are away at college and Keith has moved to California—I wake up early, with the first birds. The grey light just before dawn reminds me of Edwin's face the morning of the auction, the last time I saw him. Grey, yet light: is that the meaning of this story? I remember his hands, on champagne bottles, on children's heads, on women's arms and thighs—small hands, with that maddeningly precise angle between forefinger and thumb, the hands of the healer who makes the sacrifice.

Not, I need to say, of me: I'm flourishing in the midst of the life I've created, a life that for the first time fits. Loneliness is nothing compared to the satisfaction of a good fit.

Sometimes when I hear one of the children's voices on the telephone or recognize a friend's handwriting on a postcard or pinch back a pink petunia in the pot by my window, I think perhaps I'm becoming my own light at last—and almost too late—, one of those votive candles whose small flame sinks and rises, sinks and rises, in a crowded row at the foot of some cross.